S0-AXX-088

## Her smile bloomed. "You have a little flour…"

She pointed to the side of her nose and Zach used his wrist, the only part of his hand that wasn't covered in flour, to attempt to wipe it off.

He looked at her with his brows raised.

She shook her head. "Let me."

It was natural to turn toward her slightly.

She raised up on her tiptoes and reached out. The brush of her fingers on his nose and then his cheek was almost as light as a feather. Sensation bloomed from the place she had touched, heating his face and lighting up everything inside him.

Looking down at her like this, her eyes shining up at him, he wanted so badly to draw her slightly closer…

He threw himself out of those thoughts. He turned away so quickly that she had to step back or be knocked over.

He had to stop thinking about her like that. Stop wanting more. Grace was his friend. That was enough. It had to be, right?

**Lacy Williams** wishes her writing career was more like what you see in Hallmark movies: dreamy brainstorming from a French château or a few minutes at the computer in a million-dollar penthouse. In reality, she's up before the sun, putting words on the page before her kids wake up. When she needs to refill the well, you can find Lacy bird-watching, gardening, biking with the kiddos or walking the dog. Find bonus scenes and reader extras at www.lacywilliams.net/vip.

### Books by Lacy Williams

### Love Inspired

*The Amish Outcast's Holiday Return*

Visit the Author Profile page at Harlequin.com.

# The
# Amish Outcast's
# Holiday Return

## Lacy Williams

**LOVE INSPIRED**

INSPIRATIONAL ROMANCE

If you purchased this book without a cover you should be aware
that this book is stolen property. It was reported as "unsold and
destroyed" to the publisher, and neither the author nor the
publisher has received any payment for this "stripped book."

## LOVE INSPIRED®
### INSPIRATIONAL ROMANCE

PLEASE RECYCLE · THIS PRODUCT IS RECYCLABLE

Recycling programs
for this product may
not exist in your area.

ISBN-13: 978-1-335-56731-4

The Amish Outcast's Holiday Return

Copyright © 2021 by Lacy Williams

All rights reserved. No part of this book may be used or reproduced in
any manner whatsoever without written permission except in the case of
brief quotations embodied in critical articles and reviews.

This is a work of fiction. Names, characters, places and incidents are either the
product of the author's imagination or are used fictitiously. Any resemblance
to actual persons, living or dead, businesses, companies, events or locales is
entirely coincidental.

This edition published by arrangement with Harlequin Books S.A.

For questions and comments about the quality of this book, please contact us
at CustomerService@Harlequin.com.

Love Inspired
22 Adelaide St. West, 40th Floor
Toronto, Ontario M5H 4E3, Canada
www.Harlequin.com

Printed in U.S.A.

Therefore if any man be in Christ, he is a new creature: old things are passed away; behold, all things are become new.
—*2 Corinthians* 5:17

**For my loyal readers.**

# *Chapter One*

Zach Miller studied the farmhouse as he trudged along the gravel road toward the drive. He was trying not to think about what he'd come here to do or who was inside that house. He didn't want to chicken out.

The farmhouse and smaller building behind didn't look Amish. The house could've passed for an *Englisher*'s home, with its simple wooden siding painted white and cheery windows. It was the clothes on the clothesline—dark pants in multiple sizes and colorful shirts and dresses—along with the unhitched buggy parked beside the barn not far away that marked the property as belonging to an Amish family. He'd walked past three farms on this stretch of road that looked the same.

Each step kicked up a puff of dust and reminded him of walking home from school on crisp autumn days in the distant past.

Was this a mistake?

He hadn't considered other options. Like phoning his uncle to make sure he had a place to stay. Zach hadn't thought past what he would do when he arrived on the Beilers' doorstep.

He hadn't expected to feel this stifling weight on his chest. Sarah Beiler was inside. The woman from whom he needed to beg forgiveness. Both her and her family.

He didn't remember much from that night. Only the aftermath. He'd spent the afternoon drinking with a buddy, the same way he spent most afternoons. Or evenings, if he had to work bagging groceries. That night, Zach had chosen to get behind the wheel, even though he'd known better. And in his drunken state he'd hit an Amish buggy with his car.

The man who'd been driving the buggy died.

All because of Zach's poor decisions.

He didn't know whether the Beilers would recognize him. He'd lived in Walnut Cove, Ohio, since age ten, when he'd moved in with his uncle. But he'd attended public schools and, in most cases, the Amish didn't believe in education other than apprenticeships after the eighth grade.

And it'd been four years since his incarceration. He'd grown into a man behind bars, noticing the angles of his face in the occasional reflection from the metal mess hall tables. When he had been released this morning, he'd been given an ill-fitting pair of jeans and a button-down flannel shirt. On his walk to the bus station, he had trekked almost a mile out of his way to visit a thrift store. He hated to spend the few dollars he had on a wool coat, but with winter coming on, he'd had no choice.

During his time in prison, he'd earned a pittance. He'd spent some on his bus fare to the nearest large town and hitchhiked the rest of the way to Walnut Cove.

And now he was here. And he was terrified to knock on the Beilers' front door.

He'd had weeks leading up to his release date to practice what he was going to say. But as his feet stalled out just feet from the porch, every word he'd considered flew from his brain. How did one beg forgiveness for ending a man's life? *Could* Sarah Beiler forgive him after he'd taken away the man she'd loved?

He'd been brought up in the Amish faith. And though he'd spent years apart from the church, he still remembered how the Bible said that he should be reconciled to his brother. He figured the first step was asking forgiveness.

Behind the Beilers' barn, a grove of oaks and

maples proudly displayed their colorful leaves. Cold air nipped at the exposed back of his neck. Autumn had a firm hold on Walnut Cove, and the chill in the air was a reminder that winter was coming.

He stood for a moment too long looking at the front door. One thing he had learned during his time in prison was that putting off the difficult things didn't make them any easier. The longer he had to think about something, the more anxious he became. And so he knew this had to be his first stop after his release from prison.

He forced himself to take one step forward. And then the next. And then he was knocking on the wooden front door with a hand that trembled. It was probably a good thing that he hadn't eaten any lunch, though it was late afternoon now. The way his stomach was twisting, he might not have been able to keep it down.

He stuffed his hands in his pockets to hide the way they shook, and his right hand bumped against the smooth paper of the folded letter— the only thing he had brought with him from his prison cell.

A boy who couldn't have been more than nine or ten opened the door. His hair was slightly shaggy, falling into his eyes, and he wore a simple white shirt and dark trousers over bare feet. The boy stared at Zach curiously, and he felt the hairs at the nape of his neck prickle. It had been happening to him all day. The normal kind of interactions that he wouldn't have given a thought before his incarceration now made him feel like he was crawling out of his skin.

He had to clear his throat and swallow to get his tongue loose from where it had cleaved to the roof of his mouth. "Is your—is your father home?"

"Who is it—" A young woman appeared in the hallway behind her brother. She had dark blond hair, most of it tucked beneath her *kapp*, and at first glance, he thought it was Sarah.

But then another young woman, also with dark blond hair tucked into her prayer *kapp*, appeared, and he immediately registered the difference.

Sarah wore a navy-blue dress, and it wasn't only the difference in the dark tones of her clothing that he noticed. It was the lines of grief that bracketed her mouth. The slightly younger sister had lips that seemed to turn up slightly, as if she was just waiting to smile. Sarah's lips turned down.

His heart was beating in his throat, and he wasn't sure he could speak again. Every single word he had practiced in the solitary confinement of his cell fled.

The young boy spoke to his older sisters, and Zach didn't have to. "He's asking for *Daed*."

Sarah's face crumpled, and she whirled and disappeared into the house. Grace—it had to be Grace—smiled at him with what might be sympathy. She glanced over her shoulder to where her sister had disappeared with worried eyes.

"Would you mind waiting for a minute? I'll find out from *Mamm* when she is expecting *Daed* home." Her voice was soft and melodious, and it was such a contrast to the all-male sounds he'd experienced for the last four years that he wanted to ask her to speak again. Or maybe sing a song.

He did nothing.

She closed the door, but not before she peeked around it to look at him once again.

On her way to the kitchen, Grace Beiler glanced to where Sarah had disappeared upstairs. *Mamm* was already busy preparing dinner, her hands covered in flour as she rolled out a crust on the butcher-block counter. Behind *Mamm*, on the windowsill above the sink, were two of Grace's prize-winning violets in full bloom, a splash of pink and purple.

Grace knew who the young man was, of course. The accident had happened only a quarter mile from their home, and she and Sarah had been the first ones on the scene when Zach had been driving drunk and Sarah's fiancé had been killed. Zach's picture had run on the front page of the local newspaper after he had been charged with manslaughter.

She hadn't thought about him for a long time. She hadn't realized his sentence was up. She had not expected to see him again. What did he want, coming here?

"Can you finish chopping the carrots for me?" *Mamm* asked without looking up.

Grace edged up to the counter. "Zachariah Miller is here. He is asking to see *Daed*."

*Mamm*'s face showed surprise and then went pale as Grace's words registered. Maybe she should've softened the blow somehow. But Grace herself still felt unsettled from seeing the man on their front stoop.

He looked like an *Englisher*, with his hair cropped close to his head. And a bit like a scarecrow, with his clothes hanging off him. Had he been fed while he was in prison?

"Did Sarah see him?"

"*Jah*. She ran upstairs, probably to our room."

A little worry line appeared between *Mamm*'s eyebrows. "What does he want?"

"Elijah only said he asked to see *Daed*."

Grace hadn't been able to read the man's expression. He'd seemed closed off, except for the muscle jumping in his cheek.

*Mamm* sighed and wiped her hands on her apron. "You'd better let him in. Your father will be back in a half hour. Keep our guest company until then."

Grace knew without having to ask that *Mamm* meant to go and check on Sarah herself. It had been four years, but sometimes Sarah still seemed lost in her grief. Maybe *Mamm* would be able to offer comfort.

Zach Miller was still standing where she'd left him when she opened the door. Elijah peered out from behind Grace, trying to get a better glimpse of him, maybe. He still had his hands in his pockets, and his shoulders bunched almost up to his ears. He was handsome, she realized with a start. Had she really thought he looked like a scarecrow?

Grace realized with a shiver that a cold front was moving in.

"My father will be home soon. *Mamm* says you should come in and wait."

It was fleeting, but she caught a glimpse of vulnerability in his expression before he steeled himself again.

Whatever he had come to say, he was hiding his emotion well.

He followed her hesitantly into the living room.

"Would you like a cup of *kaffee*?" she offered.

"Maybe—maybe just a glass of water." His voice sounded scratchy, like he hadn't used it all day. Or even longer.

By the time she brought back his glass of water, Elijah and Isaiah had sneaked into the living room and were standing side by side in front of their guest.

"Who are you?" Isaiah asked with a seven-year-old's innocent impertinence.

She shooed her brothers out of the way, but of course, they didn't leave the room. That would be too easy. "His name is Zach Miller. He's here to talk to *Daed*."

Zach glanced at her sharply, then back down at his hands. Did he think she didn't know who he was?

She handed him the glass of water. He startled a little when their fingers brushed as the cup changed hands. She noticed a smudge of grease along the back of his thumb, like he'd missed a spot when he was washing up.

"When—how long—?" She cut herself off as she realized that she was being as impertinent as her young brother.

She backed away, not wanting to hover over him. She didn't expect him to answer, but he took a swallow of his water and cleared his throat. "I was released this morning."

Only this morning?

Mottled pink stained his neck, and she felt a responding blush hit her cheeks.

"Do you like to play checkers?" Isaiah asked. He sent a longing look at the cabinet behind the sofa where the checkerboard was stored away.

She got another glimpse of Zach's dark eyes as he glanced at her brother and then back down to the cup he held in his lap. Was he shy or simply uncomfortable?

"I used to play with my *daed* when I was about your age."

She was surprised to hear the German inflection come from his mouth. None of their family, none of their community, had attended his trial. They had discussed forgiving him as a community at the Sunday morning gathering soon after the accident happened. As far as their bishop was concerned, it was done. There was no need to attend the trial of an *Englisher* boy.

But was he an *Englisher* after all?

"Do you wanna play?" Isaiah asked eagerly.

Grace's heart swelled. Her younger brother was constantly looking for a partner to play with. As the baby of the family, he was always following someone around and always talking.

Zach glanced her way, and this time she was sure she saw panic in his eyes.

"I don't think—" she started.

The back door opened and closed. She heard the sound of water running as her *daed* washed up in the mudroom. Footsteps sounded on the stairs, and then her mother's soft tones greeted him. *Mamm* was talking quickly.

Grace didn't hear her father's response, but she heard his heavier tread go up the stairs.

*Mamm* appeared from the kitchen. She looked slightly flustered, color high in her cheeks. *Mamm* was the most composed person Grace knew. Except for *Daed*. Seeing her discomfited made a nervous flutter in Grace's belly. She shifted her feet.

*Mamm* glanced at Zach and then at Grace, a reprimand in her expression. "Didn't you offer our guest any *kaffee*?"

"I didn't want any." Whatever expression Zach had worn like a mask earlier had shifted now, and he looked as uncomfortable as Grace felt.

But they didn't have to wait, as only moments later her *daed* came back down the stairs, Sarah behind him. Her eyes were red-rimmed and her face pale.

Zach stood up.

"Thank you for seeing me, sir." Zach didn't seem to know where to look. His glance landed on *Daed*, then on Sarah, then back at his feet again. "I came to ask your forgiveness. Yours and Sarah's."

Zach squared his shoulders and looked directly at her father. At his side, his hand clenched into a fist.

*Daed* did not look surprised. He nodded gravely. "You have our forgiveness."

Sarah let out what might've been a gasp or a sigh.

Zach flinched, but Sarah didn't see as she left the room and fled back up the stairs.

Grace couldn't help it. Her heart swelled with compassion as she watched Zach say something else to *Daed*—his voice too low for her to hear—and take his leave. He was obviously hurting. She wanted to follow him. Wanted to help, somehow. But he hadn't asked for help, had he?

And so she only watched from the window as he disappeared down the driveway.

She should check on Sarah. Her sister must be shaken by seeing Zach. Maybe having someone to talk to would help.

But as she climbed the stairs, she couldn't forget the sight of Zach's lonely figure walking away.

# Chapter Two

When Grace came upstairs, Sarah was lying on her bed in the room they shared. Her face was buried in her arms.

The room was cozy, with handmade quilts spread across both beds. Grace had two of her favorite varieties of violets in the window, though the pair was between blooms now and only showed a profusion of green leaves. The girls shared a small bookshelf between the two beds.

"Do you want to talk about it?" Grace asked.

Sarah shook her head.

"Will you come down for dinner?"

"I'm not hungry." Sarah's voice was muffled.

Grace hesitated in the doorway, but Sarah never moved. That left Grace with no choice but to return downstairs.

After supper and some time reading in the

living room with the family, Grace excused herself to bed. Upstairs, she found Sarah sitting in the rocking chair in the corner of the room, staring out the window into the darkness. She still had on her navy dress, though her feet were bare.

Sarah didn't speak, and Grace set about getting ready for bed. She undressed and put on her nightgown. She took down her hair and sat down on the edge of the bed and began brushing the locks that extended to the middle of her back.

Sarah never said a word.

Grace missed the Sarah of four years ago. Before Thomas had died, Sarah had been a chatterbox, always full of joy and ready to share it with everyone around her. She'd always seen the good in everything around her. But after Thomas had died, Sarah had faded into a shell of the woman she once was.

The accident had been traumatic for them both. They'd been hanging clean clothes on the clothesline and heard the crash, then the scream of a horse. They'd run out into the road, and from a distance they'd seen the crumpled buggy and a red car in the ditch. Sarah had run toward the wreck while Grace had gone to their neighbor's home. The Bontragers had a phone in their barn, and she'd used it to call for help.

When she'd arrived back at the wreck, Sarah had been holding Thomas's lifeless body in her arms. By the time emergency crews arrived, it had been too late.

The firemen had had to pry Zach out of his car with a huge metal tool. He'd been unharmed except for some bruising on his face from the airbag.

For weeks, Grace had woken in a cold sweat. During the day, memories from that night would steal over her, and she would find herself blinking back tears.

Thomas's family had moved away, their grief had been so great.

How much worse had it been for Sarah?

While Grace's memories and trauma had begun to fade after several months, Sarah seemed to cling to hers. Grace didn't know how to bring her back, or if she could.

"Do you want to talk now?" she asked.

Sarah shook her head, still staring out the window.

Grace knew that her sister had to be shaken from seeing Zach earlier. When she'd opened the door and seen him standing there, it had been so very unexpected that Grace had stood frozen, not even thinking to spare her older sister from the sight of the man who was responsible for Thomas's death.

Grace should've moved faster. Although protecting her sister from seeing Zach at the door wouldn't have spared Sarah from *Daed* asking her to join the family to hear what the man had to say.

"He seemed...very repentant." Her faith demanded forgiveness whether or not the person who had wronged her was sorry, but there had been something about Zach that had touched her. Maybe it was that split second of vulnerability she'd seen on his face.

"I don't want to talk about him," Sarah said, her voice fierce. Her eyes shone with tears. "I don't want to think about him and what he cost me."

Grace put down the hairbrush and went to her sister's side, kneeling on the floor beside her. "I know it must've been hard to see him—"

"It was awful. I can't stop thinking about that day—when—" Sarah couldn't speak past the sob that escaped. She covered her face with both hands, and her shoulders shook as emotion overtook her.

Grace put her arm around her sister, holding on to her as her cries intensified and then, after a few minutes, slowly ebbed. She prayed silently, asking God to give her sister comfort that Grace herself couldn't provide. She didn't know how Sarah could still be feeling the grief of her loss so deeply. Maybe she couldn't understand because she'd never been in love, not like Sarah had been. Or maybe grief like Sarah's never went away.

When Sarah's tears were spent, Grace padded to the bathroom and brought back a damp washcloth. Sarah used it to dab at her blotchy face. She was quiet and listless, acting like a small child as Grace tucked her into her bed.

Even after Grace had doused the lamp and climbed into bed herself, she stared into the dark.

Sarah was perfectly still. Too still to be sleeping.

And then a whisper came in the darkness. "I never want to see him again."

His uncle's house looked different than Zach remembered. In contrast to the Beilers' neat yard, there was a soccer ball and a baseball mitt lying on the ground a few steps away from the front door. A tricycle lay on its side next to the driveway.

Zach felt his stomach twist uncomfortably. Had Uncle Paul gotten married while Zach had been incarcerated? Maybe he had met someone, a widow who had small children?

Uncle Paul didn't like children. It didn't make sense.

The house was run-down, with peeling paint and several shingles missing, and one shutter on the front window gone.

Memories bombarded Zach. Playing in the street, kicking a worn-out ball with a bigger boy who'd lived two houses down. His family hadn't stayed long in the rental that was even uglier than Paul's house. Mowing the postage stamp–size lawn after school on a Friday, instead of being with his friends. Paul watching TV and ignoring Zach when he needed a field trip release form signed for school.

His heart pounded. He was a man now, and if Paul was as cold as he'd always been…well, Zach had survived the last four years, hadn't he?

A tiny part of Zach couldn't help wondering if it was a mistake coming back here. He felt exhausted and wrung out from his time spent at the Beilers' home. Even walking another two miles in the near dark hadn't been long enough to erase the memory of Sarah's grief in those few moments that they had been in the same room.

It had taken everything inside him to meet Mr. Beiler's stare. The older man's expression had given no hint that his forgiving words were coming. Zach had received the words, but they hadn't lifted the heaviness from his chest. With the conviction of a teenager, he'd believed he was invincible. He'd thought he was fine to drive, even though he'd had several drinks. His decision to drive drunk had affected the whole family, but Sarah the most. And he wasn't entirely sure that she'd forgiven him, even if her father said otherwise.

Grace Beiler was the only bright spot in what had been a pretty awful afternoon. She'd shown him kindness and sort of protected him from her little brothers cornering him. She'd smiled at him. A real smile. No one else had done so.

And now he had to face Uncle Paul. With his emotions a jumbled mess.

Zach had been raised Amish, but when his parents had passed away just before his tenth birthday, Paul had come to collect him. Paul was his only living relative. And an *Englisher*.

Paul had never been warm, and Zach wasn't sure he would forgive as easily as the Beiler family had. Zach had gone from the scene of the accident to jail. From there, it had been a series of courtrooms and then prison. He'd tried to phone Paul from the jail, but there had been no answer. And Paul had never reached out once Zach had been arrested. He'd gone silent.

Maybe he didn't want to see Zach. But Zach had nowhere else to go.

He had already decided against reaching out to any of his former friends. During his high school days, Zach had fallen in with a crowd that liked to party. Zach had been so starved for companionship, and the drinking had made him forget for a little while. That his parents were gone. That he was heading nowhere fast. That Paul didn't like him.

Tiffany, his girlfriend, had been a part of the same crowd. He'd fallen fast and hard, and their relationship had gone too far. Something else his faith had convicted him of. He'd made so many mistakes.

It had taken rock-bottom and a prison Bible to remind him of the faith his *Daed* and *Mamm* had instilled in him from a young age. He'd been frightened and alone, and the Bible was the only thing that had brought him any kind of peace.

Prison had changed him. But what if his so-called friends hadn't? It was too much of a risk to reconnect. Better to stay away. Start fresh.

Uncle Paul was his only choice. Walnut Cove was so small that it didn't have a hotel. Besides, the money in his pocket wouldn't last more than a day or two if he wasted it on a hotel. Between the hitchhiking and walking from the Beilers' house, he was done in. His muscles protested the last few steps to the front door.

Seeing his uncle again was his only choice.

If Paul would let him stay the night, maybe he could figure out a plan in the morning.

When he knocked on the door, it was a young woman who answered. She appeared to be close to Zach's age, and she had a baby propped on her hip. A little girl peeked out from behind the woman's denim-clad leg.

"Can I help you?" Her voice was cool.

He could smell something delicious wafting from the kitchen behind her, and his stomach lurched, reminding him he hadn't eaten since early this morning.

"Is—does Paul Roberts still live here?"

She shook her head. "My husband and I moved in here three years ago. We rent. I don't know who that is."

Zach's heart sank. "Would you—would it be possible to connect me with your landlord? Maybe he could tell me where my uncle went."

He hadn't known that Paul rented. They'd never talked about finances, other than his uncle complaining under his breath about how much Zach ate and how high their grocery bill was.

"My husband might have the number. But he's working tonight…" She turned to speak to her daughter, who was tugging on her leg. "I know you're hungry, honey."

Zach's last speck of hope to have a warm place to sleep tonight withered and died.

When she looked back at him, the young mother was clearly exasperated at both his intrusion and her young daughter's persistence. "If you leave your number, I'll have my husband give you a call."

"I don't have a phone." The Amish didn't use cell phones. In prison, he'd found his faith again and decided to return to his roots. So he wouldn't be getting one. "Maybe I can stop by another time."

She seemed almost relieved at his suggestion. He started back down the driveway as the door shut behind him. For a moment he heard her muffled voice talking to her daughter. And then it was just him alone again in the gathering dark.

What was he supposed to do now? The prison had provided him with the name of a halfway house. But it was all the way back in Cleveland, and he was here now.

He'd been out of prison for less than twenty-four hours, and he'd already messed things up again.

It was falling dark by the time he reached Main Street. Most of the storefronts were dark, the businesses closed for the day. The cold front that had been threatening had arrived, and he stuffed his hands in his coat pockets to try and combat the chill. He should've bought a hat.

He walked by an Amish bakery and gift shop, and his feet dragged as he passed by the big picture window. Tantalizing scents of cinnamon buns or maybe sweet rolls wafted to him, and his rumbling stomach reminded him of just how long it had been since he'd eaten. His mouth watered as much as the wind was making his eyes water.

The shop was closed. The lights in the front of the store were dimmed, but in the back, half-hidden behind some shelves, he could see a young woman in a *kapp* sweeping the floor. He wondered if she would open if he knocked. Surely there was something that hadn't sold out today.

And then he remembered his dwindling cash. Better to wait.

He kept walking, praying for an idea. A place to stay.

For weeks, since his release date had been set, he'd prayed for a fresh start. He'd been raised in an Amish community in Pennsylvania, but he had no connections there now. He'd planned to see the Beilers and then stay the night with Uncle Paul. Surely one night wasn't too much to ask. Or seven. Long enough to get a job and find a cheap room to rent.

Now he had nowhere to sleep. No job. No idea what to do next.

After how his actions had impacted the community, he had no right to ask for help. He didn't even know the bishop in Walnut Cove. He might've asked the man for help if he knew where to find him.

What was he going to do?

He paced slowly up and down the street. At this time of night, there was little traffic, and no one stopped to ask him what he was doing.

In the end, he found a small space between the back entrance of the library and a garbage dumpster, where a heat register blew a tiny amount of warm air out into the night that was rapidly turning frigid. He curled himself into a ball and prayed for morning.

# *Chapter Three*

Grace had promised to help her cousin Macy and her *Aendi* Esther can apple butter the next day. The pair sold their apple butter, as well as jams and jellies, to the local bakery. It was a popular product, and she was in for a long day standing over a hot stove. The time with Macy would be a lovely change. She didn't get to see her cousin enough. And maybe Macy would have some insights on how Grace could help Sarah. Macy was intuitive and gentle and a good listener.

*Daed* had offered to take her in the family buggy on his way to the warehouse, so they'd bundled up and were now driving through Walnut Cove to *Aendi* Esther and *Onkle* Will's house on the opposite side of town.

The morning was chilly. Grace could see breath clouding in front of the horse's face.

*Daed* was silent, though that was usual. Her father was a thinker. At least, that's what *Mamm* always said. When he spoke, it was often to dispense wisdom. Others in their community often sought *Daed*'s advice. And when he spoke, it was final.

She reminded *Daed* about stopping at the library, loath to interrupt the peace of the quiet morning. She'd brought with her a cookbook she'd borrowed last week.

The building wasn't open yet, and the nighttime drop was around the corner. There wasn't room behind the building to maneuver the horse and buggy, so *Daed* pulled up to the corner and left her to walk around.

Everything was still and silent. A thin layer of frost covered the grassy area behind the small parking lot. The metal flap made a creaking metal-on-metal sound when she opened it to deposit her return. And something moved over near the dumpster.

Startled, she backed up a step.

What was it? A stray dog or some kind of critter looking for food?

And then she saw the boots jutting out from between the concrete steps and the dumpster. Surprise shifted her back on her heel. She was ready to bolt if need be. She'd never known of a single homeless person in Walnut Cove.

But whoever it was, they weren't moving quickly and certainly weren't trying to attack her. What if they needed help?

"Hello?"

A sharp breath left the person, and then their legs kicked reflexively. It only took a second for her to recognize the ill-fitting jeans. She stepped closer. The dark coat was familiar, too.

"Zach?" She wasn't sure if she dared to step closer.

He didn't seem to hear her. He didn't sit up or try to look over at her. Had he been out here all night? The temperature had dipped close to freezing. What if he had hypothermia?

She turned and rushed back to the buggy and her father. *Daed* would know what to do.

*Daed* left her holding Henrietta's bridle and watching curiously as he disappeared around the corner. He was back in what seemed like a blink, supporting some of Zach's weight. The younger man stumbled like his legs were made of wooden pegs and not flesh and bone.

*"Daed—"*

Her father kept his focus on the young man. "He needs help" was all he said.

She held the horse steady as her father helped Zach into the buggy. Zach was clumsy and uncoordinated. His cheeks were chapped with cold, and his lips were blue-tinged.

Once her father was settled and had the reins in hand, he motioned her to get in the buggy, as well.

"Grab the extra blanket," her father said.

She rummaged beneath the back bench seat and found the blanket, then climbed into the front. With Zach between them, there wasn't room on the seat. Usually Isaiah or Elijah— both of them considerably smaller than Zach— rode up front if the entire family needed to go somewhere.

Maybe *Daed* meant for it to be that way. If Zach didn't warm up, he could be seriously hurt, couldn't he?

She dropped the blanket over the front of the man beside her, registering that he was at least an inch or two taller than her father.

There was no hospital in Walnut Cove, and the doctor's office, a tiny one-man practice, wouldn't be open yet. The Bontrager family lived not far away and had a phone in their barn. Miles Culpepper was an *Englisher* who lived nearby and had a car. *Daed* could've driven Zach to either of those homes for help, but he turned the buggy in the direction they had been going, toward *Aendi* Esther and *Onkle* Will's.

"Where are we going?" she asked.

Zach's face turned slowly toward her and registered surprise. Had he not realized that she had loaded up in the buggy beside him? His dark eyes were big, and he blinked at her almost owlishly. This close, she could see a tiny scar just beneath his left eyebrow.

"We'll head to your *onkle*'s. Figure out what to do with him when we get there."

And that was that.

Since he'd gotten in the buggy, Zach had been almost unnaturally still. Maybe it was the blanket or the fact that he was sandwiched between the two of them, but he must've been warming up, because he started shivering. Whole-body shivers that rocked the buggy.

*I never want to see him again.*

Sarah's words rang in Grace's ears. She was thankful her sister hadn't come along this morning, though she'd planned to tag along until moments before *Daed* was ready to leave. She'd claimed a headache. Maybe from all the tears last night, but Grace hadn't said anything about that.

Grace understood that her sister was still hurting, but it was obvious that the man shivering beside her was in dire straits. No one would choose to spend the night outside next to a garbage bin if they had any other choice. He wasn't Amish, wasn't part of their community, but surely *Daed* would find a way to help. But wouldn't that just hurt Sarah worse?

Grace's jumbled thoughts didn't order themselves into any kind of sense by the time they reached *Aendi* Esther's.

She tied off Henrietta to the hitching post while her father helped Zach out of the buggy and to the front door. He still had the rough blanket wrapped around him.

Inside, *Aendi* Esther took one look at Zach and nudged all three of them into the kitchen. *Daed* helped Zach into a seat at the table.

A few whispered words from *Daed* and *Aendi* Esther told Grace to feed the boy. Macy was nowhere to be seen. Maybe she was helping her younger siblings get ready for the day.

*Daed* and *Aendi* Esther moved into the living room, speaking in low voices. They were soon joined by *Onkle* Will.

Which left Grace to take care of the unexpected guest.

He was silent, watching his hands that were clasped on his lap.

She made a new pot of *kaffee*. She kept stealing glances at him, aware of his rumpled appearance and the scruff at his chin.

What must it feel like to have no one to turn to for help? She'd always had Sarah. And even though she and her younger siblings sometimes bickered, she would be at their side instantly if they needed help. Not only that, but she had two sets of *aendis* and *onkles* to look after her. Plus the bishop and his family, who would find help within their church community... She was richly blessed with the people surrounding her. But Zach appeared to have no one. And it wasn't right.

She set the *kaffee* cup on the table in front of him, and he startled a little. His eyes darted to her and then back down to his lap.

"Would you like some sugar or milk?"

He shook his head. He cupped the mug between two big hands and took a sip.

Zach had been really out of it during the buggy ride. Maybe it was the warmth from being inside the house that was starting to wake him up. As soon as the first sip of coffee hit his belly, he came fully alert.

He was aware of how unkempt he must look, compared to Sarah's younger sister, Grace, in the spotless kitchen. He felt every speck of grime accumulated from being on the road yesterday and sleeping outdoors. But it was the gurgling of his empty belly registering the coffee that shamed him.

The back of his neck went hot.

Grace pretended not to notice. He covertly watched her move around the kitchen. He didn't know where they were—he'd been only partly aware—but he knew they weren't at the Beilers' home. It must be someplace familiar, because Grace moved around the room as if she was comfortable here.

The kitchen itself was clean and neat. Some kind of green plant covered in deep purple flowers sat on the sun-drenched windowsill. Several boxes were stacked in one corner, and the top one was open. He spied empty canning jars inside.

When she placed a plate of steaming scrambled eggs and two slices of toast slathered with jam on the table in front of him, he nearly wept.

"Thank you," he choked out.

He could feel her standing there, watching him. But the hunger gnawing at his belly didn't care. He shoveled several bites of the eggs into his mouth in quick succession. With her eyes on him, he felt the heat from the back of his neck settle in the spot just beneath his ears and behind his jaw.

He swallowed hard, his emotions swinging between gratefulness for the food and resentment that she wouldn't leave and let him eat in peace. He'd spent four years being watched every moment of the day.

Of course, she wouldn't leave him alone. He was a criminal, and everyone knew it. She and her father had just had a firsthand look at how desperate he was. She couldn't know that he didn't have any intention of stealing from the family that lived in this home.

This was how it was going to be now. Being watched to make sure he didn't mess up again. Making sure he didn't lapse.

She finally did leave him alone at the table as she crossed the room to a refrigerator in the corner of the room. He knew many Amish used gas-powered fridges now to keep food fresh.

*Grace.* He'd only known her by the delicate name she'd signed to a letter. But he'd imagined what she might be like if he ever got the chance to meet her in person. He'd wondered if she would live up to her name. It seemed so. She moved with an unhurried sort of serenity. He was completely out of sorts, but she seemed at peace being in the room with him, the man who had been convicted of manslaughter.

She returned to the table, this time with a glass of milk, just as he bit into the first slice of toast.

He didn't understand why she was being so kind to him. Kindness was one facet of the Amish faith, but if it had been him on the other end of that coffee mug… he would've had a difficult time serving someone who'd wronged his family.

He'd spent his time in prison readying himself to return to the Amish life—if he could find a church that would accept him. But in the face of Grace's gentle kindness, he wondered if he was ready after all.

He'd been ten years old when his parents died, but he remembered their quiet faith. They'd believed in everything the Bible said and had been a part of a vibrant Amish community in Pennsylvania before they died. He was the one who'd lost his way, living with Uncle Paul.

But Grace... Grace made it look easy. It seemed effortless for her to show kindness to Zach.

He thanked her for the milk and took a sip of it. This was not the watered-down, store-bought kind of milk that his cheapskate uncle had provided. This was the milk he remembered from his childhood, and suddenly he found his eyes swimming with tears.

He ducked his head, embarrassed for Grace to see his emotions so wildly out of control. It had to be because of the rough night he'd spent. He'd gotten very, very good at hiding his emotions in prison. He'd had to.

Again, she pretended like she hadn't seen. She moved through the sun-dappled kitchen to what must be a storage room beyond it. She returned with her arms full of the two largest cooking pots he'd ever seen.

It seemed like ages ago that he'd seen his mother in the kitchen, canning. That must be what Grace was preparing to do. Judging by the number of empty jars in those boxes in the corner, she was going to be at it all day.

"What are you making?" he asked. His voice sounded hoarse and unused to his own ears.

"Apple butter." She sent him a quick glance and smile over her shoulder. She pulled a peeler and two large knives from a drawer and laid them on the counter.

"All by yourself? It looks like a lot of work."

"I'm helping my cousin. But yes, it will be a lot of work."

She topped off his coffee cup, and he nodded his thanks.

"What will you do?" she asked.

"I don't know." He spoke to the coffee cup, feeling consternation that he still didn't have a plan. "I thought my uncle would help me, but..." But his uncle had disappeared.

"What about your friends?"

He felt a rush of the old betrayal. "The people I thought were friends disappeared the minute I got into trouble. I haven't heard from any of them in years." He'd been hurt by how quickly they'd ditched him. Especially Tiffany Boyd. They'd dated for almost a year, and he'd thought the promises they'd made were unbreakable.

But she'd dumped him via a phone call after his conviction.

He'd been wrong. So many times.

But Grace didn't need to hear about that. He ducked his head and went back to his toast.

She kept working, too. She fetched a crate of apples from the storage room and put them on a chair at the opposite side of the table from where Zach sat. But she hesitated instead of walking away.

"You should ask my *daed* if you can work with him for the day. He lost some workers over the summer, and he needs help."

And it would provide Zach with a little more cash. Maybe then he could figure out a way to track down Paul. Or whether he wanted to.

He felt a hot rush of emotion again, that she would offer this to him. Somehow he knew that if Sarah had been the daughter riding along with her father this morning, he wouldn't have eaten a hot breakfast. And he wouldn't have received the tip about possibly working with her *daed*.

He was grateful, but before he could voice it, she'd turned back to her preparations.

It was only a matter of minutes before he had cleared his plate and drained both the glass of milk and his coffee. And then Mr. Beiler joined them. His well-groomed beard and neat appearance were more reminders of how shabby Zach must look right now.

He didn't know if Mr. Beiler would give him a job today. He didn't know what he was going to do with rapidly dwindling cash and no place to stay. But at least he was facing the day with a full belly, thanks to Grace.

"Come with me," Mr. Beiler said.

Zach followed, though he couldn't help sending one last glance over his shoulder. It was probably the last time he would ever see Grace.

She gave him an encouraging smile. Her eyes sparkled with warmth, and he knew that whatever the day had to bring, he was going to hold on to the memory of that smile as tightly as he could.

## *Chapter Four*

❧

The shop was shutting down for the day. Zach had taken Grace's advice and asked her father whether he could hire on for the day, and he'd been shocked when Mr. Beiler had agreed. After a full day of working in the large part warehouse, part workshop, Zach's exhaustion encompassed every muscle. He'd forgotten what it felt like to be this active.

"*Goot* job today."

Zach looked up from putting away the mallet and chisel. Amos Graber was a nephew to Grace's *mamm* and was two years younger than Zach. Grace's cousin was as talkative as her father was quiet. Amos was one of the local men who worked for Mr. Beiler and had shown Zach around the warehouse where the team of men created handcrafted timber frames for homes and other buildings. Zach had spent the morning fetching and carrying, getting a feel for the warehouse, the tools and the work. During the afternoon, Amos showed Zach how to measure with a tape and then use a pneumatic saw to cut down wood into struts—smaller pieces that would support the frame as it came together.

Amos's ready smile and easy manner reminded Zach of Grace. He didn't know why, but he couldn't seem to keep his mind from wandering to her. It had to be because she'd provided a meal for him this morning. But somehow when she popped into his thoughts during a quiet moment, it wasn't the food he pictured. It was the laugh lines that crinkled at the corners of her eyes when she smiled. Or the gentle slope of her nose and cheeks when she'd been in profile to him.

Amos held out his hand for Zach to shake, forcing him to blink away the errant thoughts of Grace.

Zach took it. "You're a good teacher. Thank you for today."

Amos had been the first to greet Zach when he'd arrived with Mr. Beiler. Zach had understood from some of the murmured conversations in the warehouse that Mr. Beiler was never late. But he'd been late today. Because of Zach.

"Are you coming back tomorrow?" Amos asked.

Zach shrugged. "Mr. Beiler was kind enough to give me a chance today." He didn't know whether that kindness would last.

"He needs another man or three to keep up with demand." Amos's voice was low as they walked out of the warehouse and into what was left of the afternoon sunshine. It wasn't much.

"You'd be a *goot* addition to our crew," Amos added.

Zach felt a swell of some foreign emotion at the other man's words. Was Amos giving him advice, like Grace had this morning? It had been too long since Zach had experienced a real friendship. But Amos had been kind and patient all day. Was it possible a new friendship had formed?

Amos said goodbye and headed for a bicycle propped against the side of the building.

Zach saw Mr. Beiler locking up and squared his shoulders. He would thank the man for a job today. He was exhausted after a night of little sleep, but he also felt satisfied at a job well done.

Mr. Beiler looked up at Zach's approach. "It was a *goot* day."

Zach nodded. "Thank you for giving me a chance."

"Amos says you're a fast learner."

"...Thank you." He didn't know what to do with the unexpected compliment. Uncle Paul never gave compliments. Only criticized. And the prison guards certainly hadn't delivered any compliments.

Zach thought he could do the more difficult work, with some time to learn. Using the chisels was somewhat intimidating. What if he ruined an expensive piece of wood? But the work he'd been given today was well within his skills. In prison, he'd worked on engines and machinery. A repair task would be easy for him.

Mr. Beiler motioned to his horse and buggy. "Come home and have supper with my family."

Zach's movements stuttered. *What?* "I'm not sure that's a good idea." He still remembered how Sarah had run out of the room when he had visited yesterday. But another part of him warred with the anxious voice in his head. Going to supper meant seeing Grace again.

Mr. Beiler watched him with eyes that seemed to miss nothing.

"Did you find your *onkle* today?"

Zach shook his head. He'd explained to Mr. Beiler on the drive to the warehouse early this morning that his uncle had left no forwarding address. And Mr. Beiler also knew Zach hadn't left the job site at lunchtime. The warehouse was far enough from town that Zach wouldn't have had time to walk to the local library—his next idea was to do an internet search for his uncle.

The more he'd seen the way Mr. Beiler and Amos and the whole team worked together, the more Zach realized he wasn't sure he wanted to ask his uncle for help. Paul had chosen to disappear rather than sending Zach a letter at the prison. Or even making a phone call.

Zach had spent all day trying to convince himself that living under his uncle's roof hadn't been as bad as he remembered. But the camaraderie between Amos and Mr. Beiler and the others had shown him a peaceful and fulfilling way of doing things. Even at their busiest, everyone was kind and respectful.

"I don't know what to do," he said. The back of his neck went hot. He hadn't had anyone to confide in for years. Mr. Beiler had been nothing but kind toward him. But maybe it was wrong to ask for advice. The man had already given him forgiveness and a day of work.

But Zach asked anyway. "I was raised in the Amish church. But my parents died, and my uncle…" Uncle Paul had thrown away his home-sewn clothes and his boots. He'd refused to take Zach to worship, which was held in a different family's home each Sunday morning. If he'd seen Zach reading his Bible, he'd made disparaging remarks. It had been easier to put away that part of himself than to keep arguing, especially as a child.

"After…what happened four years ago, I started reading my Bible again." It was an understatement, but Zach wasn't sure he could describe how God had met him after he'd been convicted. He'd realized how very far he'd strayed from the things his parents had taught him as a child. Zach had had his eyes opened, and he didn't want to go back to that way of life. "I've returned to my Amish faith. I'd like to find a way to stay in Walnut Cove. Join a church here."

It wasn't an outright request. After everything he'd been through, Zach didn't dare ask for favors. He'd known two men from prison who had been released and ended up back behind bars within weeks. He knew that he needed a community around him. He just didn't know how to go about finding one. Or if they would accept him after what he'd done.

Mr. Beiler nodded. "Come home with me for supper. Everything will work itself out."

Zach didn't know if he could believe that. But he wanted to.

*Daed* had arrived to pick Grace up with Zach Miller in the buggy. *Daed* had only said that

Zach was joining them for supper and left Grace to make conversation on the ride home.

Sitting next to Zach filled her with awareness. She kept her gaze focused ahead but couldn't ignore his broad-shouldered build beside her.

Zach was nearly as quiet as her father. Pulling anything more than a one-word answer out of him was almost impossible. So she'd told a story about her young cousin Rachel, who'd sneaked a jar of cooling apple butter from the counter and made a huge mess in the storeroom, where she'd hidden to eat it with a spoon.

That had earned her a hard-won smile from both men.

Now they turned into the lane leading up to the Beilers' farmhouse, and she couldn't help it because she was sitting so close on the buggy seat, but she saw Zach's fingers curl into a fist on his thigh. Was he nervous after the way Sarah had acted last night? *I never want to see him again.* Sarah's words rolled through Grace's memory. She wouldn't speak out against *Daed*'s invitation that Zach come for supper, but Sarah would be emotional. Would it be hurt? Or fury?

When they rolled to a stop outside the barn, Zach offered her a hand out of the buggy. His clasp was warm and firm, and she was surprised to feel the bottom of her stomach drop out.

She turned away quickly, afraid the unsettled

feeling was showing in her expression. "I'll put Henrietta away," she said.

*Daed* nodded.

"I can help," Zach offered quickly.

She glanced at him askance. For someone who'd barely said two words the entire ride home, he was quick to volunteer.

Her father nodded again and crossed the yard toward the house.

She stood at Henrietta's head with one hand on the horse's bridle and waited. Zach looked over the harness and then back at her.

She raised her eyebrows at him.

His indifferent mask slipped again, and she saw the consternation underneath. "Can you show me? I don't actually know how this works. I just…"

"Wanted to give my *daed* a chance to go inside and warn everyone you are here?"

His mask had slipped back into place so quickly that she wondered if maybe she hadn't imagined the glimpse of emotion. "Do you think I should've stayed away?"

"It won't be easy for her to see you again. But my *daed* invited you." That would have to be enough.

Amish children were taught to respect and honor their parents. But Sarah's grief ran deep.

Grace couldn't begin to imagine what was going to happen when Zach walked through the door.

Zach's gaze cut to the road, and she wondered if he was thinking about walking back to town. Walnut Cove was so small it didn't even have a hotel. He'd already spent one night under the stars. What was *Daed*'s plan?

Before she could figure out what to say, Isaiah ran across the yard from the field behind the house. He must've seen Zach, because he altered his trajectory and headed their way.

Her youngest brother was grubby and wore a wide smile. "Hello. You're back."

"Zach is staying for supper," she said.

Her brother lit up. "Do you want to play checkers with me tonight?"

Zach looked like he didn't know how to answer.

"We'll see," she told Isaiah. "Right now Zach needs some help getting this harness off Henrietta. I don't think he's ever done it before."

Zach shot her what might have been a tiny scowl with his brow furrowed. But when he glanced back at Isaiah, his expression smoothed out. "Your sister is right. I haven't been around a horse in over ten years."

Isaiah's eyes grew round. "Really? Do you want me to show you how to do it?" Her brother's chest puffed up with innocent pride. As the baby of the family, he was often the one receiving instruction. But this chance to give it would make his day.

She held Henrietta's head as Isaiah told Zach how to unbuckle the harness. She had to stifle a smile by pressing her lips together as Isaiah recounted the entire history of Henrietta the horse and how she'd come to be a part of their family. Zach didn't seem all that rusty as he helped Isaiah lead the horse into her stall, then rubbed her down and gave her some oats.

Grace watched as Isaiah talked Zach through closing the stall gate. It was a simple latch that Zach could've figured out in an instant, but he was patient with the boy.

Zach glanced up to see her watching, and color crept up his neck.

She was about to urge them to hurry up—she was hungry after a long day of work—when Bertha, the family's farm dog, jogged into the barn.

All it took was the sight of Isaiah, and the dog broke into a run.

"Hi, girl!"

At Isaiah's exclamation, the dog started dancing around him, jumping and barking with pure joy. Isaiah leaned down to pet the collie mix and got knocked down for his trouble. Bertha took that as an invitation to lick his face up and down.

"Isaiah." Grace knew some exasperation was leaking out in her voice. Doggie kisses were not sanitary.

Zach leaned down to offer his hand to Isaiah, and since Bertha had never met a stranger, she jumped and put her paws on Zach's shoulder. He wasn't expecting it and stumbled, ending up sprawled on the floor with Bertha on his lap.

"Bertha!"

Grace stepped forward but froze when she heard Zach's laughter. He was getting the same kind of kisses the dog had given Isaiah.

And he was laughing.

His laugh sounded rusty. Like he hadn't had occasion to use it in a very long time.

Isaiah joined in, and even Grace felt herself smiling.

"She likes you!" Isaiah cheered.

Both boy and man petted the dog, ruffling her fur every which way and getting slobbered on for their trouble.

"Don't tell me," Zach said. "She's been in the family since before you were born. She went to a school for dogs and now she has a job at the library."

Isaiah dissolved into giggles. "No. She's only two. She's just our dog. And she's going to have puppies soon."

"Ah. I just thought she liked her food a little too much."

Grace shook her head at the antics of both of them. "Come along. You both need a good washing up after all of that."

Zach pushed up off the floor and straightened. "You don't like dogs?"

Bertha trotted over to sit in front of Grace, who leaned down and rubbed behind her ear. "I like them fine. I don't like being slobbered on."

Isaiah took off out the barn door at a run, probably because she'd reminded him that supper would be ready soon.

Zach neared, reaching down for one more stroke of Bertha's back. "She's a good girl," he said with his head ducked low.

Grace was surprised at the emotion choking his voice. Just as she had been to see the tears he'd tried to hide at the breakfast table this morning. Compassion welled. It was obvious he had a soft heart. Why that should be so surprising, she didn't know. It had been a long time since she'd spared him a thought. Years. And back then, she'd thought of him only in terms of what he'd done. The drunken teenager, a party boy. The man who'd killed Thomas. The prisoner.

She had never thought of him as a man with hopes and dreams and hurts of his own.

When he straightened again, he gave her a tight smile, and she saw that his indifferent mask was back in place.

But as they walked together to the farmhouse, where her family was waiting, she couldn't help remembering her glimpse of the man underneath.

# Chapter Five

Zach followed Grace's lead and washed up at the sink in the mudroom.

It wasn't easy to follow her through the kitchen door, but he did. Nerves twisted in his stomach. Would he be welcomed?

Mrs. Beiler smiled at Grace, but her smile faded as she encompassed Zach with her glance. She only nodded at him. Perhaps that was his answer. Tolerated, but not welcomed.

Grace glanced uncertainly from her *mamm* to Zach. He pretended not to see as he dried his hands.

Two sisters in identical lilac dresses wearing white aprons carried dishes from the kitchen to a long plank table in the next room. Mr. Beiler had mentioned Verity and Violet, twins, but Zach wasn't prepared for the glances that darted his way. Neither daughter quite met his eye, which reminded him of other prisoners in his cell block.

He followed Grace out of the kitchen and into the dining room. The table already had a leaf in and was clearly meant for eight. One extra chair threw off the arrangement. Just like his presence.

Grace's younger brothers were already seated. They bickered in low voices but went silent when Mr. Beiler entered the room.

Zach's heart beat in his throat, and he wondered whether he would be able to force down any food. The emptiness in his stomach that had bade him accept Mr. Beiler's supper invitation had now been replaced by what felt like a writhing pit of snakes.

Grace sent him a tentative smile as she led the way to the table. It made him think back to the moments in the barn when she had laughed at the dog's antics. He didn't know her. Not really. Only through a few scrawled words in a letter from years ago.

But she seemed such a joyful person. In the barn, for one moment, all of the turmoil inside him had settled. The combination of Grace, Isaiah and the dog had brought him a sense of peace.

That was gone now.

If he couldn't sit through one dinner with the Beiler family, what hope did he have at staying

in Walnut Cove? Or making a true home anywhere? He'd always be branded an ex-con, no
matter where he ended up. Whatever came his
way tonight, he was determined to bear it. Even
if it meant apologizing to Sarah again.

He slowly approached the table, still following in Grace's footsteps. Mr. Beiler and the
boys were in their seats. A shadow shifted in
the hallway, and he realized someone was standing there. Sarah.

Grace hesitated, her face turning toward the
hallway.

He opened his mouth to offer to leave. If the
girl couldn't even sit down to eat dinner with
her family, he should be the one to go.

But before he could say anything, Mr. Beiler
said, "Zach. Join us."

He was stuck. He refused to offend the man
who had offered him a job for the day and a hot
meal. He sat down next to Grace. Isaiah leaped
up from his seat across the table and scurried
around to sit at Zach's side. He gave his brother
the stink eye, but Zach didn't know why.

Mrs. Beiler and the twins joined them at the
table, carrying the last bowls. The table was
spread with a hearty stew, extra helpings of veg-
etables and the biggest golden dinner rolls Zach
had ever seen. His stomach clawed at his insides, aching for a taste.

Grace made quiet introductions around the table. Zach nodded at the twins, though neither one quite met his eye.

Finally, Sarah walked out of the hallway and sat at the other end of the table, as far away from Zach as she could manage. She pointedly ignored him, and he felt his stomach sour.

The family bowed their heads in silent prayer, and Zach followed suit.

His prayer was a wordless cry for help. Help out of this awkward situation. Help that he could know the right thing to say.

As movement around the table signaled that others had finished giving thanks, he looked up. Right into the face of one of the twins who was staring at him directly. Verity.

She quickly dropped her eyes.

He averted his gaze and was happy to accept a basket of rolls when it was offered to him.

It was easier to keep his eyes on his plate. He had a difficult time swallowing the stew, though it was delicious.

Violet asked Grace about her work at the Grabers' home, and Grace chattered about the same mishap with her young cousin that she had regaled him and Mr. Beiler with on the drive home. She seemed agitated, speaking quickly and gesturing with her hands.

No one else seemed to notice. They chuckled at her anecdote.

All except for Sarah, who ate in silence. And Verity, who refused to look at Zach at all.

He had grown accustomed to being ignored during his time in prison. Sometimes it was a blessing. Other inmates always seemed to be angry. Even an imagined slight was enough to cause trouble. Zach had been very careful to keep to himself and stay out of trouble as much as possible. Right now, he felt as nervous as he had when another inmate threatened him. His heart was pounding. His palms sweated.

When the conversation hit a lull, it was Elijah who spoke. "*Daed*, is Zach gonna keep working with you?"

"I hope so. Zach is a diligent worker."

Unexpected gratification suffused Zach's cheeks with heat. Today, he had felt like he couldn't find his feet as he had tried to learn the ropes. But if Mr. Beiler thought he was a good worker, then that was something, wasn't it?

Elijah spoke. "Why do I have to keep going to school? I want to go work with *Daed*."

This seemed to be a familiar discussion, because Mrs. Beiler sighed. "Schooling is important. You have only two more years before you are finished."

Elijah argued, "But *Daed* can teach me everything I need to know at the shop. I don't like school."

Zach froze for a moment at the boy's audacity. He and Uncle Paul had had too many shouting matches during Zach's teenage years. Zach never won. And after Paul had finished having his say, he would give Zach the silent treatment for days.

He braced for whatever might come, but Mr. Beiler kept eating, as calm and unhurried as before.

Elijah's chin was jutted out stubbornly.

Next to him, Isaiah was eating as if he'd skipped lunch. Violet and Verity were having a whispered conversation, and Grace was watching Sarah.

Zach was so uncomfortable, he wasn't certain he could finish his food.

Grace could feel the coiled tension in the man beside her, noticeable since Elijah had first argued with *Mamm*. Before the argument, Zach had been eating much like he had eaten breakfast this morning—like it'd been weeks since his last meal, not hours. When Elijah had talked back to *Mamm*, Zach had gone completely still, almost as if he anticipated something terrible happening. She didn't know why.

If only Sarah would say something, it might

ease some of the heaviness. But even though she'd been trying to catch Sarah's eye since she'd sat down at the table, Sarah seemed determined to ignore everyone.

*I never want to see him again.* Whatever Sarah was feeling, she was hiding it. For now. How could Grace smooth things over?

Verity, too, wore a frown. Grace's younger sister was extremely shy. They frequently had company, but friends and family that Verity was comfortable with was different than having a stranger at their table. Verity would hate the attention.

"You can work in the shop on Saturday," *Mamm* told Elijah.

"Maybe you can show Zach how to use the pneumatic saw," Isaiah piped in.

The innocent statement from her youngest brother seemed to break the hush that had fallen over the table.

Zach had stiffened slightly. Now he cleared his throat and spoke to *Daed*. "You cannot know how much I appreciate that you want me to keep working for you, but I...cannot. I have to find a place to stay."

Was it pride that kept him from accepting?

He glanced surreptitiously down the table. At Verity or Sarah, she didn't know.

But a pit opened up in Grace's stomach.

She couldn't forget the moment she'd seen him this morning, huddled behind the library. How desperate must he have been to sleep there? She turned beseeching eyes on *Daed*, but he was considering Zach with a steady gaze.

"We have the *daadi haus*. It is sitting unused." *Daed* gave Grace an apologetic glance. The living room of the smaller house was filled with her flowers. "Almost unused. You should stay with us until you get back on your feet."

Sarah slammed her fork on the table. "You can't let him do that!"

Zach's expression was no longer carefully blank. Now it showed his discomfort. "Mr. Beiler, I can't accept your kindness."

For once the boys were quiet, their eyes wide.

*Daed* spoke into the awful silence. "Do you have anywhere else to go?"

Zach shifted his seat. "No," he admitted.

Grace's heart broke a little for him.

"You are welcome here. At our table—" he sent a quelling look at Sarah "—and to stay in the *daadi haus*."

Sarah stood, her lips trembling. It was clear that Grace's prayer for her comfort had gone unanswered. "You cannot ask me to share a table with him."

Zach flinched as if struck.

Sarah's face was mottled pink now. Her anger

showed in her clenched fists and set jaw. She stared at Zach, demanding something. Grace didn't know what.

Why didn't *Mamm* interrupt? She was focusing a little too intently on her plate. Grace held her breath, wanting to say something. Not knowing what.

"I'm sorry," Zach said. "I—shouldn't have come."

"That is enough," *Daed* said. His jaw was clenched, and he looked furious. His expression was one that Grace had never seen before. "We will not speak of the accident again. What happened is over and done."

Sarah stared at *Daed* with tear-filled eyes. *"Daed—"*

But *Daed* shook his head, his lips in a firm line.

Sarah rushed out of the room and upstairs.

Zach shifted in his seat. "Maybe I should go."

"But you promised to play checkers with me after supper," Isaiah protested.

Zach looked unsettled at the reminder and glanced at Grace as if for help. Gone was the man who'd laughed helplessly in the barn. Now his eyes told her he was burning up from the inside out.

Her gaze swept to the stairs, where Sarah had disappeared. Sarah didn't want Zach here.

But Sarah hadn't seen his desperation this morning.

Grace smiled at him. "It would be a shame if you left now. *Mamm* made apple pie. I can bring your piece into the living room while you play with Isaiah."

The wrinkle of his brows said he wanted to refuse, but Isaiah had his hands clasped beneath his chin with a pleading gaze.

"I'll stay for a little bit."

*Daed* nodded. "Fine."

Isaiah scampered off into the living room, and Elijah was quick to follow. "I've got next game."

Zach looked discomfited but slowly rose and followed her brothers.

Grace helped *Mamm* and Violet clear the table. *Daed* and Verity went upstairs. Grace hoped *Daed* would talk to Sarah and that her older sister would listen to what he had to say. Sarah's outburst was out of character, even in her grief. Sarah wasn't cruel, but her words had been.

*Mamm* sent Violet into the living room with a piece of pie for Zach. *Mamm* was strangely quiet, frowning down at the sudsy water as she scrubbed the plates that Grace brought her.

After the dishes were washed and the table

scrubbed clean, *Mamm* asked Grace to check on their guest.

She stood in the doorway for a moment, watching. The living room was surprisingly quiet. Isaiah's head was bent over the checkerboard, his nose scrunched up as he considered his next move. Several checkers of both colors were scattered on the table next to the board. Isaiah appeared to be winning. Zach had barely touched his pie.

No one had noticed her, so she used the opportunity to study Zach. He was in profile to her. While both her brothers fidgeted, always filled with energy, Zach was perfectly still. He watched Isaiah with quiet, patient intensity. He wasn't relaxed, she realized. His posture was too straight—one hand was clenched on his knee. As if he was nervous.

If he was anxious, why had he stayed? Only because Isaiah had begged for a game? He hadn't wanted to disappoint her brother, and that endeared him to Grace.

"I should've warned you that Isaiah would show no mercy," she teased softly from the doorway.

Zach glanced at her briefly but didn't smile.

"Would you like some *kaffee*?" she asked.

"No, thank you."

"I want some pie," Elijah said.

"With milk!" Isaiah piped up.

She shook her head. "You know *Mamm* won't let you eat in here."

"Let's pause the game," Isaiah said. He and Elijah hurried out of the room toward the kitchen. Which left Grace and Zach alone. She moved into the room and leaned against the back of *Mamm*'s favorite chair, a wing back angled toward the center of the room.

Zach stood and pushed his hands into his pockets. "I should go."

She thought again of Sarah and what her sister would think. But she couldn't hold back the words. "You should reconsider. *Daed* meant his offer of a place to stay."

He shook his head. "I can't stay here."

"Then where will you go?"

He scowled, but she didn't think it was directed at her. He was struggling with difficult circumstances. "I don't know." He sounded almost angry.

"Do you want to find your *onkle*?" He'd mentioned the man this morning. "Maybe staying here is your answer," she suggested. "Why not stay for a few days while you search for him? You could ask around in town. Surely someone must know where he went. Or you could try using the computer at the library."

For the first time since she'd come into the

room, he let himself really look at her. His intent gaze made her heart pound.

"You…are not what I thought you'd be like."

She was confused. She'd seen Zach at the scene of the accident. He'd been in the back of a police cruiser, his head down. But they'd never met before yesterday when he'd showed up on the doorstep. "What do you mean?"

"You sent me a letter, not long after I was convicted. You probably don't even remember." He dug in the pocket of those ridiculous jeans and pulled out a piece of paper that was folded and worn from being handled.

And it came to her in a quick rush. She *had* sent him a letter. In those first months, she'd sat with Sarah in her grief. She'd thought about the young man who had done this to her family. She'd been angry, working through her own grief.

"I don't remember what I wrote," she said now. Had she been as cruel as Sarah was tonight?

"You said you were praying for me. And that you hoped I found faith."

That didn't sound terrible.

"Your words reminded me of my parents. They were Amish. And I knew that they would've been ashamed of me for walking away from the faith they'd instilled in me as a child."

It was the most words he'd spoken in the few interactions they'd had. She realized she was holding her breath, imagining the boy he'd been.

"Your letter brought me back to the faith."

Surely it couldn't be as simple as that. "You want to join the Amish church?"

He nodded, but he'd grown uncomfortable again. He was seemingly unable to hold her gaze, his eyes downcast.

"You should stay," she said firmly. "*Daed* can introduce you to our bishop. Maybe even study with you."

His gaze shifted to her again, and she saw a glint of hope. "But your sister…" His words trailed off. A muscle jumped in his cheek.

She would speak to Sarah. Surely her sister would understand that Zach was different now. He wanted to join their church. He'd come to them to make amends. If she explained, surely Sarah's fury would settle. Wouldn't it?

Zach needed a place to stay. And he needed a friend. That much was clear.

"It will work itself out," she said.

*Daed* seemed to think so. Had he known that Zach wanted to join the church? That was a reason for him to invite Zach to stay.

And maybe it would be enough to change Sarah's mind about Zach.

## Chapter Six

"Zach will stay."

Grace looked up from the notebooks she'd spread across the dining room table.

Zach stood slightly behind *Daed* in the living room doorway. She'd left him to finish his checkers game with Isaiah when the latter had barreled back into the room, shortly after their conversation. *Daed* had joined the males a while later, and soon after, both her brothers had raced up the stairs to their bedroom, leaving *Daed* and Zach to talk.

Grace knew this because she'd been working in the dining room. She hadn't been eavesdropping, but her brothers were noisy, and it was easy enough to guess what they were up to. *Daed*'s and Zach's voices carried to her, though she couldn't hear their words.

*Daed*'s words registered. Zach was staying.

"*Goot*," she said. Her eyes met Zach's briefly over *Daed*'s shoulder.

"Would you take him over to the *daadi haus*?" *Daed* asked.

"Of course. I'll need a few minutes to clean up my mess."

*Daed* clapped Zach on the back and headed into the living room. His nightly routine was to read the Bible before he retired to bed.

She scooped her notebooks into a pile and led the way into the mudroom, where she bundled into her coat. The *daadi haus* was only across the yard, so she didn't put her mittens on. She grabbed a flashlight from the storage bench and turned it on.

Darkness had fallen and she was aware of the breadth of Zach's shoulders as he followed her out the back door. She shivered against the cold that slapped her cheeks and crossed her arms over her middle.

At the sound of their footsteps on the porch, Bertha roused herself from her favorite resting place beneath and came out to greet them.

Grace kept walking, but Zach stopped to give the girl a pat. He spoke quietly to her before he straightened and then jogged to catch up with Grace, though he kept more distance between them than one of her friends might.

The flashlight beam bobbed on the ground in front of them.

"She'll start following you around if you don't watch out," Grace said.

"That's okay. I always wanted a dog growing up."

"Your uncle never let you have one?"

He shook his head, and the slight smile he'd worn after petting the dog disappeared. "He thought they were too much trouble. Or maybe I was trouble enough."

What a terrible thing to think. Isaiah and Elijah could be frustrating at times, but they'd never been made to feel unwanted.

The night was cold and quiet around them. She didn't know what to say in response to Zach's quiet confession, and then the smaller house loomed out of the shadows, distracting her.

It had been built for *Daed*'s father when *Daed* and *Mamm* started filling the bigger house with children. *Mamm* liked to tease Isaiah about her and *Daed* moving into the *daadi haus* when he grew up and inherited the big house.

"My *grossdaadi* died three years ago, and the *daadi haus* has been empty since," she said. "I've been using the living room as a makeshift greenhouse, but no one has touched the bedroom. It'll need to be aired out."

She pushed through the door into the kitchen, where a kerosene lamp waited on the counter. Zach stood in the doorway, still keeping several feet between them. Did he think she was frightened of him?

Rather than juggle the flashlight and matches, she held out the flashlight to him. "Here."

He had to take a step closer to take it from her. She reached for the box of wooden matches. There was a soft *whoosh*, and the pungent scent of sulfur permeated the room as she lit the lamp wick.

"There's a battery-powered lamp in the living room," she said. "And the bedroom, too, I think. I'll bring some fresh batteries over in the morning."

Zach remained an arm's length away. He'd set the flashlight on the kitchen's island counter and now looked around the room that was filled with soft yellow light. The lamp cast shadows and made the planes of his face sharp. Maybe he'd been smooth-shaven yesterday, but tonight whiskers darkened his jaw. She glanced away from him, attraction making her belly dip.

He took in the room, and she tried to see it through his eyes. One wall was made up of cabinets, upper and lower, with a countertop between them. The sink was beneath a window that looked toward the big house. A breakfast nook in the corner was the only place to eat in the *daadi haus*. A darkened hallway led to the bedroom, and a doorway next to it led into the living room.

Everything was of good construction but minimally decorated. Her *grossdaadi* had been a man of simple tastes. Her *grossmammi* had died long before Grace had been born.

Zach swallowed hard.

She rushed to fill the silence. "It's only dust. A *goot* scrubbing will set everything to right."

"It's fine." His voice was hoarse, and he turned his head so she couldn't see his face. "It's more than I need. More than I expected."

*Oh.* Compassion swelled, but the last thing she wanted to do was embarrass him. She pretended she hadn't seen his show of emotion.

"The bedroom is through there." She motioned to the hallway. "Sheets and a quilt should be in the chest at the end of the bed. Let me clean up the living room and then I can help make the bed."

"I can do it."

She nodded and left him to find the bedroom on his own. She took the flashlight into the living room.

The earthy scent of soil and growth hit her. It usually brought a smile, but tonight she grimaced, because she caught sight of the boxes of empty plastic pots that had arrived yesterday. They were stacked haphazardly in the center of the room. She'd forgotten about them. The boxes weren't heavy, but the four-inch pots took up a lot of room, mostly because of how many she'd ordered.

*Daed* let her run her own small business. She'd sought his advice in the beginning, but as she'd gotten her feet under her, she'd needed him less and less. *Daed* didn't know how her inventory had grown or how many supplies she'd put up in anticipation of Christmas orders that would come in over the next few weeks.

"Whoa."

Zach's voice from behind her startled her slightly. She tried not to show it, turning to smile at him where he stood in the doorway. He held the lamp, which illuminated what the flashlight's beam couldn't.

"I found the blankets," he murmured. "I was coming to see if you needed help."

"I was going to stack everything up, but…" There were too many boxes. Zach wouldn't be able to use the room at all. "I will ask *Daed* if I can move some of these out to the barn." She indicated the boxes at her feet. Not only were there the pots, but she used a special kind of potting soil, and there were several large boxes of that. And shipping supplies. Empty boxes, plastic to wrap the violets in, tape. She had a system.

"If we stack them against the wall, you'd at least have room to walk through here," she said.

He put the lantern on a small table next to the sofa. The sofa itself had been pushed back against the wall and covered with a white sheet to preserve it. Then he joined her in stacking the boxes against the opposite wall.

She loved the shelves in front of the picture window. Her father had custom-built them for her last summer. Each level was built to look like three stairs, so the flowers growing at the back wouldn't be blocked by those at the front.

As Zach helped her, she caught him glancing at her several times. He always dropped his eyes, but it didn't stop her cheeks from filling with a blush.

The boxes stacked, she moved to scoop up some loose empty pots and a trowel. She'd long ago spread a thick plastic drop cloth across the floor to protect it, and it crinkled under her feet.

Zach had moved to the shelves and peered at the tray of baby plants that were crowded together and growing fuller every day. She needed to transplant them to their own pots soon.

"I think I saw one of these plants in your aunt's kitchen," he said. "What are they?"

"African violets. A popular houseplant," she added when he sent her a curious glance.

"You sell them in town?"

"I have displays in several stores, but most of my sales are through internet orders. I ship all across the country. An *Englisher* friend helped me with the online stuff." She'd been friends with Haley since elementary school, though their friendship had moved out of the classroom after eighth grade. Haley had helped her put up a store on a popular craft site, and an unexpected blessing had come when Grace's violets had been featured in the website's weekly email. She'd sold out her stock, and orders had kept pouring in.

"They're pretty," Zach said.

"Thank you. They make good gifts. If you take care of them, they will bloom all year long." She pressed her lips closed. Surely he didn't want to hear all the details she could spout about houseplant care.

She made her tone businesslike. "I can move the boxes out of here tomorrow, but the plants will have to stay."

"I don't mind the boxes. I'll probably only be here a couple days, anyway." Now he was glancing past the plants outside the darkened window. What was he thinking about, that his jaw had locked up like that?

It would be convenient not to have to tote all her supplies from the barn when she needed to repot or ship plants.

"Why don't we compromise? I'll move some of my extra supplies out of the way."

"Fine." He nodded to the shelves. "It looks like you're about to outgrow your space."

She pulled a face. "I've been pestering *Daed* to build me a greenhouse. Not a large one." She gestured with her hands, though that wouldn't do justice to the ten-by-ten building she imagined. "But he's been very busy in the shop since he lost two employees this summer." More information than Zach needed to know. She cleared her throat. "I'll have to come in and water the plants every other day. I'll try to do it when you're not here, so I don't bother you."

His expression turned incredulous. "Please don't worry about bothering me. I'm the one intruding in your life. Yours and your family's."

Her mind's eye provided a picture of Sarah's stormy expression as she'd run from the table earlier. And then *Mamm*'s fierce frown as she'd scrubbed the dinner dishes. But she couldn't erase the memory of Zach's husky voice saying, *It's more than I expected*, and the turn of his cheek so she wouldn't see his emotion.

"We are happy to share with you what God has given to us."

His skepticism remained, but he only nodded.

She moved across the room, toward the kitchen and the back door beyond. "*Daed* likes to get an early start in the mornings. There's no food here. You should come up to the house and eat breakfast."

Zach ducked his head. "Maybe."

She took the flashlight with her as she moved through the kitchen. Her hand was on the doorknob when he called out. "Grace!"

She turned to where he stood in the shadowed doorway, across the room. "Thank you. For everything."

Her cheeks heated. *"Willkumme."*

She rushed across the chilly backyard and into the house. There was still a lamp lit in the living room, and she went inside to say goodnight to *Daed*.

He looked up from the Bible in his lap. "Zach settled in?"

*"Jah."* She lingered behind the chair. "Is Sarah—Will she be all right?"

*Daed* laid his hand on the open pages of his Bible. "Sarah must find her way to forgiveness, or the bitterness in her heart will take root."

"What can I do for her?" Grace wanted to take action, wanted to erase Sarah's pain.

"Pray. She needs prayers from all of us."

But after she'd crept into her room and readied for bed, after she'd slipped under the covers as Sarah slumbered—or pretended to—it was Zach that her heart lifted in prayer.

Zach made the bed. He stood over it for several minutes, looking at the hand-sewn quilt and the soft pillow. So different from the uncomfortable cot in his barren cell.

He left the bedroom to prowl through the darkened house. It was small but comfortable. Far more room than he was used to. He stood for a moment examining the plants that had made Grace light up when she'd told him about them.

Each plant boasted deep green leaves. A couple dozen were bursting with purple, pink and white flowers. Others were clearly adolescents, smaller as they worked to fill out their pots. Grace's shelves were overflowing, with some pots balanced close to the edge of the simple wooden frame. She would gain more room when she shipped some out, but he could see by the tray of seedlings that her space would be quickly used up again as she potted the growing plants.

In her own way, she was filling the world around her with beauty. He'd noticed the plant in her aunt's window. It was easy to imagine her plants in windows all over town. All over the county and farther.

It wasn't only the plants that created beauty. It shone from Grace herself. He'd had to turn his face away more than once, uncomfortably aware of the gentle winsomeness of the woman herself. He'd been afraid of making her nervous, been careful to put distance between them. Sarah's dislike was palpable. He didn't want to do anything that might make Grace's kindness disappear.

What had he been thinking, showing her the letter he'd kept during his incarceration? He patted his pocket now, making sure it was still there. Her letter had challenged him to come back to his faith. It was the only thread that had connected him to the Amish community in Walnut Cove. And it was the only breath of kindness he'd had during the years in prison.

The letter hadn't been his reason for coming here. But maybe it had been part of the draw. He'd wanted to meet the young woman who'd written it.

When he'd spoken with Mr. Beiler, Grace's *daed* had encouraged him to stay as long as he'd needed. He'd been surprised when Zach had brought up his desire to join their house church. He'd offered to go speak to the bishop with Zach. It was another blessing Zach hadn't expected.

He moved into the kitchen, curiosity driving

him to open the cabinets. Cooking pots in the lower cabinets. Plates, bowls, cups in the upper. A neat stack of dish cloths and a handful of home-sewn hot pads in two drawers.

Not a scrap of food. It wasn't a surprise. Grace had indicated as much when she'd invited him for breakfast.

He glanced out the window over the sink. The big house was visible just across the yard. A soft light shone through one of the lower-level windows. The upper windows were dark.

He didn't know whether he could face Sarah across the breakfast table. He knew that God had forgiven him for what he'd done. And Mr. Beiler had granted a blanket forgiveness from their family.

But it was clear that Sarah was still furious and that Zach's presence upset her. The last thing he wanted was to cause pain in this family that had offered him so much kindness over the past day and a half.

He would stay for a couple of days and find another place. Surely it wouldn't be that difficult to find his uncle, now that his immediate need for shelter was taken care of.

And he wouldn't go to the big house for breakfast. He could skip one meal. Tomorrow, he'd stop at the grocery on the way home. A jar of peanut butter and a loaf of bread would last him a couple of days and wouldn't eat into his meager cash supply too badly.

It was more of a plan than he'd had yesterday. Yet he still felt unsettled.

He went back into the bedroom. He found a Bible, cracked with age, in the drawer of the nightstand. He was careful with it, not wanting to inadvertently damage it. It must've belonged to Grace's grandpa.

He spent a half hour squinting in the soft lamplight—so different than the fluorescent lights he'd been accustomed to—reading the New Testament. Being in the Word had given him the only sense of peace he'd known for the past years, and it did the same now.

After he'd washed his face and lain down in the cool, soft sheets, he stared up at the ceiling. There had to be a way he could repay the kindness the Beilers had shown him. It had started this morning with the breakfast Grace had made for him. Mr. Beiler hadn't had to give him a chance working in his shop. Then supper and a place to stay. The debt was piling up, and Zach was determined to find a way to pay it back. He was rusty dealing with animals. Isaiah had shown him around the barn, but Zach felt he would be more hindrance than help if he tried to help there.

If only they had a car that needed repairs.

During his stint in prison, Zach had worked in a program that taught auto repair. Tools and engines had become a language he spoke easily. But, of course, most Amish communities didn't believe in their families owning automobiles.

He would have to find another way.

He rolled over on his side. Sleep seemed far away. The bed was so much softer than what he was used to. The house was too quiet. He'd grown accustomed to snores of other men, weird metallic sounds, guards talking to each other.

It was his own disquiet that made it hard to sleep.

He had prayed for so long to be released, but he still felt the same deep loneliness that had haunted him behind prison walls.

Would it never go away?

He longed for a family of his own. For someone to belong to.

For a moment, his mind presented a memory of Grace, smiling at him.

He crushed that thought.

Grace wasn't for him. She was from a good family. She was sweet and kind.

He was responsible for taking a man's life. He'd taken Thomas's chance at having a family.

She probably pitied him. He couldn't allow himself to read more into it.

He would never deserve someone like Grace.

# *Chapter Seven*

Grace went through the motions as she and Verity carted boxes from the family buggy into the tiny Walnut Cove post office. She'd spent the morning packing up a dozen violet orders that had come in over the past week.

And trying to come to terms with the argument she'd had with Sarah several mornings ago. She'd woken early enough that dawn was barely lighting the horizon out the bedroom window. Sarah was already up, donning her apron over a pale blue dress. She'd glanced out the window, and Grace could guess what she'd seen by Sarah's gasp of outrage.

"What's *he* doing here?"

Grace had still been in that pleasant place halfway between sleep and waking, but at Sarah's words she sat up. Sarah must've seen Zach in the yard. What was he doing up so early?

Grace hadn't had a chance to talk to her last night, and she'd hoped for a more peaceful setting to orchestrate the conversation. Not first thing, when her brain was still muddled from sleep.

She brushed a hank of hair out of her face. "You heard *Daed* invite him to stay in the *daadi haus*. Zach accepted."

Sarah's back was to Grace, and she couldn't see her sister's expression. But Sarah had let the ties of her apron fall to her sides, and her hands were shaking.

How could Grace make her understand?

"Zach wants to join our church," Grace said softly. "I think he is very different from the person he was four years ago. He changed."

Sarah sent her a sharp glance. "You would judge that from one suppertime conversation?" Her words cut like shards of glass.

Grace swallowed back words that would explain that she'd spent more time with Zach last night as he'd settled in. She considered her words carefully as she threw back the quilt and got up. "Would you have *Daed* turn him away?" He didn't have anywhere else to go.

"*Yes.* Every time I look at him, I think of that night. It was— I can't—" Sarah shook her head.

And Grace remembered her own nightmares and the memories that had taken months to fade.

How could she ask Sarah to forget? What right did she have to tell Sarah her grief was wrong? None.

"*Daed* should have found somewhere else for him to stay. Why should I have to see him every day?" Sarah slammed her hairbrush onto the dresser with a loud crack.

Grace jumped. She hadn't even realized Sarah had been holding it.

"It's not fair!" Sarah cried.

*Couldn't you try to give him a chance*? Grace didn't dare say the words waiting on her tongue. Not when Sarah was this upset.

"You're on my side, aren't you, Grace?"

Grace was so lost in what she should've said or what she might say that she didn't know how to answer. She swallowed hard. "*Schwester*, I love you—"

Sarah nodded as if that settled it in her mind. "I knew you would see things as I do. Zach doesn't belong here."

And Grace was so shaken by the conversation that she hadn't had an adequate response before Sarah had left the room.

The whole thing had left her feeling unsettled. And not long after, she'd been on her way to the chicken coop to gather eggs. Zach was crossing the yard to meet *Daed* by the buggy. They were on their way to work, probably. Sarah's words in Grace's muddled mind had made her duck her head instead of calling out a *goot* morning to him.

And he hadn't been back to the big house in the days since he'd come to stay in the *daadi haus*.

"Grace? Grace."

She blinked and realized both Verity and the postman were looking at her questioningly.

"Do you want expedited shipping?" Verity asked, and Grace had the feeling this wasn't the first time the question had been uttered. She'd been so lost in her thoughts that she hadn't noticed.

"Not today," she murmured.

It only took a few moments for them to complete the transaction and walk back out into the afternoon sunshine.

"What's the matter with you today?" Verity asked. "You've been distracted."

"I have?"

Verity leveled a look on her. "You spilled milk all across the kitchen floor, and you had to redo two of your packages because you'd mixed up the flowers."

They crossed the street to the grocery. *Mamm* had asked them to do the week's shopping, as they had to drive the buggy to make Grace's deliveries.

When Grace hadn't answered, Verity lowered her voice. "Is it because of Zach?"

Grace hoped she sufficiently hid the surprise from her expression. Verity was intuitive. But she'd also witnessed Sarah's outburst on that first night, and they had a new guest in the *daadi haus*.

And Grace couldn't talk about her early-morning conversation with Sarah. Not when her emotions were so conflicted.

"What do you mean?" she hedged.

"You and Sarah are close. She's been upset ever since *Daed* asked Zach to stay. I thought maybe she'd said something to you."

Grace shook her head. "Not much."

She did love Sarah. They'd been as close as could be since she was a toddler and could follow her big *schwester* around. But Sarah was wrong about Zach.

Wasn't she?

Grace couldn't forget Zach's hard-won, hesitant smile. Or the vulnerability he'd shown when he'd said that he'd always wanted a dog but was never allowed to have one.

Did she want Sarah to forgive him because she was drawn to him?

Zach left early to work with *Daed* each morning, and the two men didn't return until well after dark. They'd obviously gone somewhere after work each night, but she didn't know where.

She wanted to talk to Zach. She wanted to know how he liked working for *Daed*. She wanted to know if he'd been searching for his *onkle*. If he was eating.

But she also felt the pull of loyalty to her sister. If she was friendly with Zach, it would hurt Sarah.

So she'd done nothing.

Inside the store, Verity was distracted by choosing a cart from the row and then fishing *Mamm*'s list from her apron pocket. She pushed the shopping cart down the dry goods aisle, but Grace stumbled when Verity abruptly turned the basket around and scooted past the end of the aisle.

"What—?"

"Shh!" Verity shushed her with a frantic wave, and Grace followed her sister, though she couldn't resist throwing one look over her shoulder.

She caught sight of him just as she turned the corner and joined Verity, who stood half-hidden behind a display of handmade soaps. Caleb Stolzfus.

He'd been the bane of Verity's existence during their school days. It had only gotten worse after that. He had moved away from Walnut Cove two years ago. So what was he doing here?

"Did he see you?" Verity whispered.

Grace was opening her mouth to tell her sister how *verrickt* she was acting—surely the man was past foolish pranks now—when someone spoke from behind her.

"What are you doing?"

Verity jumped, but when Grace turned, it was their cousin Amos and his younger sister Susanna.

Greetings were exchanged and all the while, Verity stretched her neck as if she couldn't help looking for Caleb.

"How are things at school?" Grace asked Susanna. The girl would turn thirteen in the spring, so this would be her last year in the classroom.

Susanna pulled a face. "Miss Troyer didn't like one of my essays and pre-algebra is more difficult than I thought it would be. My grade is *baremlich*."

"Wasn't Verity the top of her class in pre-algebra?" Amos asked.

Verity had turned her head and was staring down the nearest aisle with fierce concentration.

"Yes, she was." Grace used her elbow to nudge her sister. "Verity, maybe you could tutor Susanna."

"What?" Verity shook off her distraction to rejoin the conversation. "Oh. I'll ask *Mamm* if I can ride over on Saturday. We can study your algebra then."

"Verity? Is that you?"

Grace's sister tensed up as Caleb Stolzfus abandoned his half-full shopping cart to join them.

"Hello, Grace. And Amos and Susanna. Good to see you."

Grace accepted the handshake from Caleb. She hadn't seen him in two years, and the man she remembered as being a slightly gangly teenager had filled out considerably. His dark hair curled beneath the brim of his hat. His easy smile was the same as she remembered.

He turned it on Verity, who had crossed her arms and wore a frown. She didn't see his smile because her gaze was fixed on his midsection.

"What are you doing here?" Verity asked stiffly.

Susanna watched the interaction with wide eyes, but Grace didn't hear Caleb's answer, because Amos pulled her aside.

"How d'you like Zach?" he asked, his voice for her ears alone. "Miller," he added. As if she wouldn't know who he was asking about.

Zach again. She was already conflicted over the situation with Sarah, and Amos's question just made it worse. She tried to smile. "We haven't seen much of him the past couple nights. Why?"

"He's a fast learner and a *goot* worker. We may finish the Wanner job on time if your *daed* keeps him on."

Some of the tension gathered in her shoulders released. "That's *goot*."

Amos's brows furrowed. "What's the matter?"

Her cousin was too perceptive. "Nothing."

"You don't like him?"

Grace was aware of Susanna, watching and listening to everything.

"I like him fine," she said stiffly.

Amos raised his brows now. "You *like* him?"

Sometimes she wanted to pinch her cousin. Maybe he could tell, because he rocked back on his heels.

She hadn't told anyone that she was drawn to Zach. She glanced back to Verity, hoping for a distraction. But her sister still stood with closed-off body language. Caleb didn't seem to notice as he regaled her with a story about…rescuing a goat from a barn fire? Susanna was watching the entire thing with rapt attention.

"Did you hear about *Aendi* Martha?"

Amos's question brought her attention back to

him. Thankfully, he wasn't asking about Zach any longer.

"What happened to *Aendi* Martha?" Martha was Grace's *mamm*'s aunt and owned an apple orchard on the other side of town.

"She fell and broke her leg. *Mamm* was going to ask *Aendi* Beth if one of you girls could stay with her for a few days."

"I hadn't heard."

Caleb finally walked away, and Verity looked at Grace with her lips pressed together in a fierce frown.

"I'll let *Mamm* know," Grace told her cousin. "I think we've got to finish our shopping now."

Verity was already marching ahead, pushing the shopping cart. Grace rushed to catch up with her.

Zach banged his knuckles on the bottom edge of the Beilers' wringer washing machine. He hissed in a breath and brought the bruised hand up to press against his lips.

He'd removed the drain pump from the washer here in the Beilers' basement. The expansive room was lined with shelves along one wall, all of them filled with canned goods. The washer and a sink with a deep reservoir were on the wall perpendicular. Two card tables were surrounded by chairs in the center of the room, and Zach had a sense that it wasn't usually this quiet down here.

For a half hour, the only sounds had been the clank of his tools and his own breathing.

He still wasn't used to the quiet after his stint in prison. He was a little surprised one of Grace's younger brothers wasn't down here spying on him or bugging him. Maybe Mrs. Beiler was the only one who knew he was down here. She'd been the one to let him in the back door when he'd knocked, not long after he and Mr. Beiler had arrived home from the shop.

Zach had been ready to duck inside the *daadi haus* and spend the evening alone, when Mr. Beiler had asked him if he could try and repair the family's washing machine. A repair like this one wouldn't even make a dent in the debt Zach owed the man. How could he say no?

But the last thing he'd wanted to do was go inside the big house. Not when the last time he'd seen Grace, she'd turned her head instead of greeting him.

After her kindness in helping him settle in at the *daadi haus* the night before, he'd been surprised and...hurt by her avoidance. His pulse had beat in his cheeks as disappointment rolled over him. He'd spent the entire quiet ride to Mr. Beiler's shop telling himself it was what he should've expected. Had he really thought she would welcome a friendship with him?

He'd spent the past three evenings with Bishop Zook and Mr. Beiler. They'd quizzed him on his Bible knowledge and also studied with him. They'd asked questions about his renewed faith and why he desired to join the church. The questions they had asked him about his future plans were more difficult to answer. He wanted a place to belong.

Sometimes he still felt like the ten-year-old boy who'd landed on his uncle's doorstep, unsure of his welcome.

Mr. Beiler and Bishop Zook seemed satisfied with his Bible knowledge. But if he wanted to join the Walnut Cove church, he would have to be a part of the church and community for some time. After several months, he would meet with the bishop again, and then it would be put to a vote.

Maybe he should've gone to another Amish community. Maybe he still could. He had almost a week's pay saved up after Mr. Beiler had paid him in cash each evening. Surely Bishop Zook and Mr. Beiler would make a few phone calls and help him find a place to stay.

Except… Zach was beginning to feel as if that would be throwing Mr. Beiler's kindness back in his face. Not many ex-cons got a chance like the one Zach had. It was an unexpected blessing.

Mr. Beiler had insisted Zach stay for supper after he fixed the washing machine. Zach hadn't been able to say no, but he'd secretly hoped the repair would take longer. All night, even. Then Zach wouldn't have to sit across the table from Grace in uncomfortable silence. He also couldn't forget Sarah's angry tears. Would she still be furious at his presence? She had every right.

The washing machine wasn't cooperating with his plan to stay in the basement all night. The repair was straightforward, not like working on an auto engine. Zach hadn't counted on the minerals accumulated on the drain pump connections. He'd spent a little time wrestling with the wrench to get the pump off. Now it was only a matter of attaching the new pump and putting everything back together.

He sighed. It was going to be supper with the Beilers after all.

As if his thoughts had summoned her, he heard Grace's voice on the stairs. Someone was with her.

Anxiety tightened his gut, but it was Verity who was arguing with her older sister. Not Sarah.

"…He's foolish and I can't stand him."

He let his wrench clank on the edge of the washer. He didn't want to surprise them.

Grace looked up, meeting his eyes as she traversed the last step. She had her apron gathered in front of her, carrying something wrapped in its skirt. When she saw him, her eyes widened. He waited for her to glance away, but she didn't.

Verity nudged her sister when she didn't move, and Grace stepped out of her way. "Zach. *Goot daag*," Verity said.

"Hello." He nodded.

Verity moved to peruse the canned goods stacked on the shelves on the far wall. Grace was still staring at him, and his cheeks began to burn.

"You look different," she said.

So he did. He could almost pass for Amish now.

Mr. Beiler had introduced him to a young widow in the community. She'd been willing to part with her late husband's clothing, and Zach had paid her to make alterations so the pants would fit. Being back in homespun felt a little surreal.

He'd also bought a pair of suspenders and a hat.

Zach knew that his hair would have to grow before he would really look the part. And it would take more than looking Amish for him to truly fit in.

He turned his attention back to the repair as Grace crossed the room to a shelf only a few feet away from him.

*Be a friend.* Mr. Beiler had encouraged him to make friends in the community. The problem was…he was badly out of practice. He didn't count anyone from prison as a friend. He'd kept to himself, and once he started rediscovering his faith, most of the other inmates hadn't wanted anything to do with him.

The adolescent friendships he'd had before prison hadn't lasted past his court date. Not even his relationship with his former girlfriend, Tiffany, had survived.

He wasn't sure he knew what true friendship looked like. And he wasn't sure Grace wanted to be his friend.

He cleared his throat. "Are you…having a good day?" That was awkward. He closed his eyes against the embarrassment of it.

But when he heard movement from Grace, he dared to look up. She smiled at him. She was emptying her apron of a pile of wooden clothespins. Two fell out on the floor, and she bent to whisk them into the bin on a shelf.

"Yes. Today is a *goot* day."

He felt bolstered by her smile.

"Your new best friend, Bertha, has been missing you," she said.

Grace's mention of the dog made him chuckle, the sound as rusty as it felt. "I've missed her, too. I'll be sure to say hello when I leave."

Verity stepped closer and both girls looked at the washer parts he had strewn across the floor.

"*Mamm* will be thankful for you fixing the washer," Verity said. "Elijah and Isaiah dirty a lot of laundry."

"I'm happy to do it. I learned how to do repairs in—in prison." He faltered over the words. He'd meant to offer something about himself but clearly hadn't thought it through before he'd started speaking. He'd rather that part of his past be forgotten completely.

"I'm sure *Daed* appreciates your skill at the shop, too," Verity said. "He had to pay a handy sum last year to have a repairman fix one of his saws." She showed Grace two glass jars. Grace shook her head, and Verity crossed the room again to put the jars back on the shelf.

Grace stepped closer to Zach. "Do you need any help?"

He shook his head. "Getting the old pump off was the hard part. It won't take long to put this back together."

He wasn't looking directly at her, but his peripheral vision caught the way her gaze lingered on his face. "*Goot*. If you're almost finished, you can stay for supper."

He didn't mention that her father had insisted he stay.

"We've been taking guesses as to what you might've been eating," Verity said over her shoulder. "Has it been only bread and water?"

She was teasing him. Somehow, her teasing didn't light him up inside the way he felt when Grace gifted him with one of her smiles.

"Close," he admitted. "It's been too many peanut butter sandwiches. And I could use a break from them. If you're sure it won't make things difficult. For—for the family." He meant to say *Sarah*, but he couldn't quite get her name out.

Grace and Verity exchanged a glance. Grace was the one who spoke. "Our *aendi* broke her leg, and Sarah's gone to stay with her for a few days."

So Sarah wouldn't be at supper. He felt relief and guilt in equal measures. Now he could fulfill his agreement with Mr. Beiler and not worry about upsetting Grace's sister at the same time. Maybe it was selfish on his part, but he couldn't help his relief.

Grace seemed to sense his turmoil. She smiled gently at him, and his gut pinched. "You are *willkumme* at our table, Zach. The boys will want to hear all about your work this week. Be prepared to play at least one game of checkers after the meal."

"Do you play?"

He regretted the question when Verity glanced their way. Grace looked uncomfortable.

"Grace likes to play word games," her sister offered. "Scrabble. Boggle." She crossed the room again and held up two more jars. Grace nodded this time.

"Do you like those games?" Grace asked.

"I don't know. I've never played them." His uncle had never owned a board game. And Zach was no wordsmith. But if Grace asked him, he would try.

"Maybe we can talk *Mamm* and *Daed* into playing with us," Grace offered. "Pictionary or charades."

Verity grimaced, and Grace laughed. "She hates charades," she told Zach.

"I don't like it when people stare at me," Verity muttered. She turned her back and walked to the stairs, leaving the two of them behind.

Grace was looking at Zach in a soft way that made his skin feel too tight. He ducked his head, remembering the way she'd turned her face from him before. Better not to hope for too much.

"It will be a fun night," she said.

He nodded. One night was enough. How could he ask for more?

# Chapter Eight

"Keep it steady, there."

Zach felt the pull in his muscles as he and several other men braced the frame for one wall of the house they were raising. At the corner of the new structure, Mr. Beiler and two other men fit together the frame and added thick wooden pegs to secure it.

It was a mild Saturday morning, and the entire Amish community in Walnut Cove had gathered for the house raising. Mr. Beiler's crew had provided every piece of wood for the frame. Zach and the others had spent the past two days outdoors on the property, fitting together the frame for both ends of the house flat on the ground.

In the two weeks since Zach's arrival, he'd spent most of his working hours helping prepare for today. Job Zook was a distant cousin of

Bishop Zook and had contracted Mr. Beiler to both supply the frame and run the house raising.

Zach couldn't believe how many folks had shown up to help today. When Mr. Beiler had informed him about the event, he'd thought it would be the five of them that worked in the shop who showed up today.

He couldn't have been more wrong.

Every family in the community was here. Buggies and bicycles lined the road.

Men swarmed like ants over the job site. Once the two ends of the house were secured and the frame for both sides was completed, they would raise the trusses for the roof and connect those, as well. With so many hands, the house would be framed in a matter of hours.

"I'm late. Don't tell *onkle*." Amos came alongside him, his ready smile familiar to Zach after so many days working together. He moved into place, standing a shoulder-width apart from Zach.

"How could he notice in this chaos?" Zach asked.

Amos wrinkled his nose. "He notices everything. Mmm. I think I can smell apple pie from here."

Zach shook his head at his friend's antics. Amos was always hungry.

"How can you not be famished? Look at all that bounty." Amos nodded to the spread.

Job Zook's new house was centered in a large, open field. Sawhorses had been spread and planks laid across them to make temporary serving tables away from the new house. They'd been covered with fabric tablecloths, and once the raising was completed, the tables would be filled with delicious, home-cooked food. Everyone would picnic together.

Zach wasn't sure he should stay.

He figured he could slip away from the gathering without attracting attention. *He notices everything.* Amos's words replayed in his mind. Zach had ridden over in the buggy with Mr. Beiler this morning. His boss would notice. And Zach didn't have a ready excuse.

Mr. Beiler gave the all clear, and Zach was free to let go of the two-by-four he was supporting.

He and Amos followed the team around the foundation, ready to lift the other side of the structure. When the command came, the group of men lifted the top of the framed wall and then walked forward, pushing it until it was upright. Mr. Beiler and his helpers moved into place to attach the strong wooden pegs.

"Any luck locating your *onkle*?" Amos asked.

"I'm getting good at running internet searches.

But there's no record of Uncle Paul anywhere in the county." Thus far, he'd restricted his search to the small towns nearby. His uncle had always complained about the big city, so Zach hadn't run his search there yet. Paul Roberts was a common enough name that even searching the records in a small town took time.

Last Tuesday evening, he'd bicycled to the rental house where he'd lived with Paul. He'd given his name and the Beilers' address to the young mother—still no sign of her husband—and asked if she would send him the contact information for the landlord. Her baby had been crying, and she'd been clearly impatient, so he wasn't holding out much hope.

He was beginning to wonder if he should give up.

At that moment, Grace passed by the opposite side of the structure. With only the frame in place, Zach had a clear view of her. She had two little girls by the hands, and all three were chattering and giggling as they walked. She looked up, her eyes landing unerringly on Zach.

She smiled, and his stomach performed some kind of gymnastics, twisting and flipping.

Grace said something to the two little girls, and they both looked at him and waved before they walked on.

Of course Amos noticed. When Zach glanced

at him, he wore a smirk. "I told you on Sunday to ask if you could walk her home next time."

Zach had attended worship with the Beilers every other Sunday since he'd arrived in Walnut Cove. During his first Sunday, at the urging of Bishop Zook, he'd stood up in front of everyone there and made a public apology. It had been one of the most difficult things he'd ever done. He'd been choked up with tears by the time he was finished.

Last week, he'd allowed himself to be talked into staying for the evening event, a time when the young, single people sang more lively songs— still a cappella—and socialized.

At first, Amos was kind enough to introduce him around. When Amos was at his side, Zach received smiles and handshakes. But when Amos had been drawn into a private conversation with friends, Zach had been left on his own.

And it was clear from the suspicious glances that he received that he wasn't entirely welcome. Everyone knew everyone else. These were teens and young adults who had grown up together. They'd known one another since they were babies. They'd gone to school together. Some of them were clearly paired off, though Amos had informed him that most couples kept their courtships private until they married.

Zach was the outsider. He might be dressed like everyone else, but that didn't mean he fit in.

He used a quiet moment to covertly watch Grace. She and her sister Violet didn't lack for male attention. He didn't see Verity, but that was probably because he couldn't seem to look away from Grace. She'd been full of laughter, joy radiating out from every smile.

And then she'd noticed him standing alone.

When she joined him, two men who'd been talking to her sent him glares that could only be construed as protective.

Zach knew that someone like Grace must have a half-dozen beaus. Or maybe even a boyfriend. Someone upstanding, respected in the community.

Not someone like Zach.

But when she asked, "Will you sit with me?" he found himself agreeing. He hadn't even realized that the group was circling up in the unfamiliar basement.

He sat next to Grace in a folding chair that was too close. His shoulder brushed hers, and he couldn't have said whether she'd asked him a question. The songbook felt foreign in his hands, but Grace was already turning pages.

And someone started singing. Voices raised around him, and he was aware that he was the only one not singing. The only one who didn't know the tune or the words.

But Grace smiled at him when he began to hum along. She'd also smiled at her sister across the room. And several other people. It didn't mean anything special. She was kind to everyone.

"She rode home in Jacob Troyer's buggy," he reminded his friend now.

Amos made a soft *pffft* sound. "She rides home with someone different every week. She doesn't want to hurt anyone's feelings."

That wasn't comforting. It meant she probably didn't want to hurt *Zach's* feelings. He wanted to scowl at the wood in front of him, but he kept his face carefully blank. It wasn't Grace's fault that he was thinking about her far too much.

Grace had a special kind of warmth about her. It was there in her smile, in her steady gaze. When she looked at him, he felt as if she could see right into the heart of him.

She was a…friend? And he refused to do anything that could threaten that.

Amos could tease all he wanted. Zach knew his place, and it wasn't beside Grace.

He caught sight of her fair hair beneath her *kapp* again. Or thought he did. When he turned to look, his gaze snagged on Sarah. He quickly averted his gaze. He hadn't known Sarah would be here today. Of course, she would attend. He hadn't seen much of her since she'd gone to stay with her great-aunt. Today's house-raising had drawn the entire community.

But the sudden lurch in his stomach was a reminder that the last time he'd been in her presence, she'd been furious and upset. Maybe this was the excuse he needed to give Mr. Beiler. He didn't want to ruin today's event for Sarah.

After the prayer to bless the food, Grace had helped her young second cousins fill their plates and ushered them over to their mother.

When she returned to fix her own plate, the crowd had thinned. She glanced around, scanning the grounds for Zach. She'd thought perhaps he would be with Amos and his friends but didn't see him there.

Where was he?

There. Standing between two buggies with a plate of food. What was he doing over there? Didn't he have a place to sit?

But she was distracted by the sight of Sarah and Verity, who seemed to be having a whispered argument over the pasta salad. Her stomach twisted. She'd known Sarah was coming today. She'd thought she was prepared to face her sister.

But the nerves in her stomach belied that thought.

Days ago, when she and Verity had come across Zach in the basement, she'd seen his uncertainty and shyness. And her heart had gone out to him. Sarah was gone, visiting their *aendi*. What would it hurt if Grace befriended him?

But now, faced with her sister's presence, she was afraid Sarah wouldn't understand.

No use fretting about it. She crossed to her sisters.

"*Goot daag*, Sarah."

Sarah's eyes were shadowed, but she accepted Grace's hug. "Hallo."

"*Vee bisht doo?*" Grace asked.

"I'm fine." But Sarah's lips were pinched, and she looked unhappy.

"How's *Aendi* Martha?"

"Her leg is doing much better. But she's come down with a cough, and I don't like the sound of it."

"Oh, no."

"Hallo, Sarah. And Grace and Verity."

Grace turned to greet Dan Glick across the serving table. He wore a pale blue shirt that made his eyes even bluer. He'd been Thomas's best friend, and sometimes it had been the four of them playing games or taking walks together. Thomas and Sarah, Dan and Grace.

Thomas and Dan had been as close as brothers. They'd gone fishing together on a rare afternoon off. Thomas had ribbed Dan, an only child, in a good-natured way about not having younger siblings around to annoy him.

For a short time, she'd thought that maybe Dan would come courting...but after Thomas's death and everything that had followed, she'd rarely seen him.

His attention was on Sarah as he asked about the family.

Verity leaned close to Grace. "Where's Caleb sitting?"

This again? Grace resisted the urge to roll her eyes. "With his family, I'm sure."

Verity scanned the gathering. What did she have against the man? Sure, he'd embarrassed her in their school days, but that was long ago.

"May I drive you home in my buggy?"

Grace had been peeking back in the direction she'd seen Zach and was only half aware of Dan's question until Sarah suddenly gripped her hand, hiding their clasped hands in the folds of Grace's skirt. Her clasp was so tight it was a warning.

"Not today. I've been staying with my *aendi* and must spend some time catching up with my family."

Dan looked between Sarah and Grace as color

climbed into his neck. He nodded, clearly disappointed.

And Grace squeezed Sarah's hand back. "Another time?" she asked. "I'm sure Sarah would love a chance to catch up with you, too."

Something sparked in Dan's eyes, and he nodded. He excused himself.

Sarah let go of Grace, whose stomach was rumbling, reminding her it'd been a long time since breakfast.

"Why did you do that?" Sarah asked.

Grace didn't answer immediately, reaching for a plate from the table. She began to fill it. Sarah did the same, Verity behind her, still distracted by her search for Caleb. There were only stragglers remaining, everyone else already eating.

"Grace," Sarah prodded in a whisper.

"Taking a drive might be a good thing." She didn't look directly at Sarah as she piled her plate with food. Was she really going to do this? She was. "Dan is a catch. Every girl in Walnut Cove would say yes if he asked. And…wouldn't Thomas have wanted you to be happy?"

Thomas hadn't been the kind of person to hold a grudge. He'd once forgiven a young Isaiah for scratching up the paint on his brand-new buggy.

She heard Sarah's intake of breath, felt her sister stiffen beside her.

"Why don't you go with him then?" Sarah asked in a terse whisper.

Almost of its own accord, Grace's gaze went to Zach.

And Sarah's eyes must've followed. Suddenly, she grabbed Grace's wrist in a painful hold.

"Sarah, let go." She tried to shake off Sarah's hold, but her grip was too tight.

Sarah's eyes were suddenly bright with tears.

"He needs a friend," Grace said quietly. She looked around, afraid they were drawing stares. Verity had faded away somewhere. Maybe she was hiding from Caleb. No one seemed to be looking at them.

"He doesn't need you. *I* need you. You're my sister."

Sarah's words hit like a physical blow. Of course their relationship was special.

But Grace's gaze was drawn to Zach again. He was still hiding halfway behind one of the buggies. Because he thought he didn't belong? Or had no one invited him? That wasn't right, either.

"What harm can it do to share one meal together?" she asked.

Sarah's jaw set in a stubborn expression Grace recognized. "It can harm you. Zach Miller isn't what he seems."

What? Grace's confusion must've shown on her face.

"I don't trust him. He can dress like one of us, but that doesn't mean he is one of us."

"Sarah—"

"I ran to town yesterday evening to get *Aendi* Martha some medicine for her cough, and I drove the buggy right by him on the sidewalk. He was talking to one of his old *Englisher* friends. He's up to no good."

Grace shook her head. "How do you know it was one of his friends? It could've been someone on the street who stopped him for directions."

Zach had been a stranger to them when the accident happened. She doubted Sarah had any memories of who his friends were back then.

Blotchy color swept into Sarah's face. She looked around and must've realized where they were. She let go of Grace abruptly.

"Can we talk later?" Grace asked.

Sarah stormed away without answering.

Grace stood with her plate in hand, unsure whether she should follow Sarah. Or approach Zach.

*He can dress like one of us, but that doesn't mean he is one of us.* But Zach had attended worship with the family. He'd spent time studying with *Daed* and Bishop Zook. Grace had spent enough time with him to know that he wasn't the monster Sarah believed he was. He was a kid who'd made some bad choices and he'd paid dearly for those choices.

Of course she cared about Sarah's feelings. But she also had compassion for Zach. When she'd seen him on Sunday evening, he'd been standing alone. He just needed someone to draw him into the circle. Her friends were kind. They would welcome him.

Now decided, she gripped her plate and set her feet in Zach's direction.

He watched her approach and lowered his plate down in front of him. She saw that he'd already managed to devour half of his food.

"You must've worked up quite an appetite this morning," she teased gently.

He looked down at the plate, almost as if he was surprised to see the food gone.

"Everything is delicious. So much better than—"

He cut himself off. She realized he must mean the food he'd eaten in prison. Maybe he didn't want to talk about it. Or maybe he thought she didn't want to talk about it.

"You'll want to save room for my rhubarb pie. There are never any leftovers."

He answered the smile she had given him

with one of his own and then ducked his head
as if bashful.

Her stomach was gurgling with hunger.
"Come sit with me and my friends. You met
some of them last Sunday."

He kept looking at his plate. "I don't know if
that is such a good idea. I'm…bad with names."

Did he mean that? Or was he unsure about
joining in?

"No one will mind. I promise. C'mon… I can
be just as stubborn as Isaiah when he wants you
to play checkers."

His gaze came up, his eyes searching hers.
Finally, his lips moved in a reluctant half smile.
"I suppose I don't have any choice then."

She was relieved when he followed her. She
chose a seat among her friends, a mix of men
and women. Zach's knee bumped hers as he
settled on the very edge of the picnic blanket.
Having him near made awareness zip down her
spine. She'd noticed the same thing sitting beside him during the singing last Sunday.

To distract herself from the pulse thudding
in her ears, she made introductions around the
picnic blanket.

"We met last Sunday," Elmo Bontrager said
with a nod.

Miriam Troyer leaned forward. "You're staying in the Beilers' *daadi haus*, right?"

Her brother Benjamin chuckled. "Isn't that where Grace keeps all of her plants? I think I would have nightmares of them suffocating me. Vines growing until they trapped me…"

"I don't have any vines and you know that, Benjamin Troyer," she said tartly.

There was laughter all around, and even Zach smiled. His gaze cut to Grace's and then away. Connection sparked again. Heat climbed to her cheeks, and she didn't know if it was because she was being teased or from Zach's smile.

He gave a tiny shrug. "I like the plants. They're pretty. For a long time, I didn't have much beauty in my life."

Was he talking about his time in prison? Or before that? From the little she'd gleaned when he'd mentioned his *onkle*, the man couldn't have been easy to live with.

She didn't want the conversation to become awkward, so she quickly jumped in. "My violets are beautiful and *wunderbaar*."

Someone groaned.

Miriam cringed, but it was all a tease. "Watch out. She's going to lecture us about her plants."

Grace rolled her eyes at the good-natured ribbing.

Zach didn't seem fazed. "I like to hear about *wunderbaar* things."

"You've done it now." Benjamin pretended to plug his ears.

Maybe he was right. Grace wrinkled her nose. "They've already heard all this before."

"Oh, go ahead," Miriam said.

"Well, if one of the leaves becomes broken and I need to remove it, I can plant that leaf in soil and it will grow a new plant. So even if a violet is badly damaged, it still has life. It may take months or maybe even years, but there is still beauty in the plant. It just has to grow."

Zach looked up, and their gazes caught and held. He looked so different from the day he'd landed on her doorstep. It wasn't only the clothes. He'd lost the look of a scarecrow. He filled out his clothes better. He'd lost the haunted look in his eyes. A few weeks of being in Walnut Cove had changed him. His outward appearance now better matched the man beneath.

What would he be like in a few years? Planted in the community...would he grow into a confident, strong man?

She had to look away when he held her stare too long. Was he holding his breath, too?

Conversation flowed around them, moving on from Grace's violets. Zach cleared his throat and looked down at his plate. "I'd like to buy one of your violets."

She studied his hat, since he seemed determined not to meet her eyes again. "I'll give you one."

He shook his head, but she was determined.

"I've got to go get some of Grace's rhubarb pie," Benjamin said.

Joseph Glick quickly stood, joining him. "Zach, you'd better come quickly. You don't want to miss this."

Zach sent a grateful look to Joseph and joined the men as they made a beeline for the dessert table.

Verity sank down into the place Zach had just vacated. "Caleb Stolzfus is driving me crazy. He won't stop following me around. Do you think *Mamm* and *Daed* will let me go stay with *Aendi* Martha instead of Sarah?"

Grace studied her sister. Verity didn't look flushed and pleased by the attention. She looked tense and stressed. "Maybe *Mamm* will let you both go."

"And stick you and Violet with all the chores at home?" But Verity's eyes were narrowed as if she could see how it might work.

Grace's gaze slid toward where Zach stood with Joseph and Benjamin. The three of them chatted near the dessert table. For once, Zach looked relaxed.

She didn't realize Verity was speaking to her until her sister nudged her.

"Hmm. You're distracted again. Now will you admit that it's because of Zach?"

Grace's face flamed. "I'm not—"

Shaking her head, Verity laughed. "You don't fool me. Not anymore."

Grace couldn't deny it. Not truthfully. She was drawn to Zach.

Maybe if Sarah came home, Grace could talk with her sister more. Somehow, she had to make Sarah see the man Zach was now.

Because Grace couldn't stop thinking about him.

# Chapter Nine

Two weeks passed. December arrived with a blustery snowstorm, and Bertha gave birth to five healthy puppies.

Saturday morning, Zach stopped in the Beilers' barn to check on the new mama and her two-day-old pups. He sat on his haunches and watched from outside the partition Isaiah and Elijah had rigged up to keep Bertha inside one of the empty stalls. One of the pups was curled in a ball, deep asleep. The others wiggled and piled on top of each other as they nursed. The tiny coos they made arrowed straight to his heart, though he didn't try to get closer or pick one up. That would come later. Right now, they didn't even have their eyes open, and Bertha was right to be protective of them.

Footsteps alerted him that he wasn't alone, and he looked up to see Grace striding toward him, lugging a pail of what must be fresh water for the new mama.

He straightened and reached for it. "Here. I'll get it."

She turned the heavy pail over to him. Their fingers brushed in the exchange. Her touch was gentle and unfamiliar, but he still jerked away from it.

She didn't seem to notice as she smiled at him. He felt her smile deep inside, the way she lit up from within as if seeing him filled her with joy.

Everything inside him seized up. His attraction to her had only grown bigger after the picnic. He couldn't stop thinking about her.

He forced himself to cut his eyes away after only a second. He turned away so he could lift the pail over the partition. He removed the old one, with only dregs of water left in it. That bought him only a few seconds.

It was terrible to be so drawn to Grace. He had tried willing away his attraction to her. He had tried praying it away.

But no matter what he did, he couldn't seem to stop thinking about her.

"Have you been out here all morning?" Her question was filled with gentle teasing. "I think it's safe to say that only Isaiah has checked on the puppies more than you."

Her teasing tone warmed him, but she couldn't know how true her words were. He *had* been hiding in the barn. Sarah had returned home two days after the house raising, while Verity had gone to stay with the girls' great-aunt. Sarah's presence had brought a tension that even Isaiah and Elijah noticed.

And Zach didn't want his staying here to make things difficult for Grace.

She moved beside him, closer than he would've allowed himself to stand. Close enough that he got a whiff of cinnamon and sugar, as if she'd baked something delicious and sweet for breakfast.

She peered into the stall, and he found himself fascinated by a strand of hair that caught on the slope of her cheek. He forced his eyes back to the dogs and not the woman.

"I can't believe how small they are," he found himself saying. "I thought they'd be bigger."

She seemed content to watch the puppies snuggle together. Their cries quieted.

And Zach tried to soak in this perfect moment. Tried not to want more. Grace must think of him as a brother, or a friend. She treated him just the same as one of her friends. Like Benjamin, who'd escorted her home in his buggy from the Sunday evening singing last week.

Zach had been fiercely jealous, though he had no right to be.

Grace wasn't for him.

He'd made so many mistakes. Mistakes that weren't erased by an apology or even by his time in prison. He would face the consequences of the choices he'd made for his entire life.

And he deserved every one of them. Every narrow-eyed glance. Every time he was left out of being invited to a gathering. Every ounce of hatred that Sarah held for him.

Maybe he didn't deserve Grace's kindness. But that didn't keep his parched heart from soaking up every drop of it. His heart wanted to trick him into thinking it meant more.

She turned her face to look at him. "Maybe *Daed* will sell you one."

It took him a moment to remember what they'd been talking about. His heart leaped at the idea of having one of Bertha's puppies for himself. He'd always longed to own a dog, a companion that would be happy to see him. Like Bertha herself, who greeted him with a wagging tail and a doggy smile.

But he quickly crushed the hope. He kept his eyes on the now-sleeping pups as he shrugged. "I don't even have a home for myself. It probably wouldn't be the best idea to get a dog." No matter how much saying the words caused a sudden ache in his throat.

"Did *Daed* ask you to vacate the *daadi haus*?"

"No. The opposite, actually." When he'd brought up finding another place to live, Mr. Beiler had looked at him askance and asked if he was planning to leave Walnut Cove so soon.

"I offered to pay rent," Zach said.

Grace sent him a sideways glance and laughed a little. "He said no?"

Zach nodded. "I don't know how I'll ever pay back the debt I owe to him." He glanced at her and then away. "To your entire family." His insides knotted just thinking about it.

Mr. Beiler had given him more than a place to stay and a job. He'd given Zach a chance to start over and a hand of friendship. It was more than he could've hoped for, but he couldn't depend on the Beilers' charity forever.

Grace turned toward him and parked one hand on her hip. He turned to face her. When she spoke, she sounded almost angry. "There's no debt, Zach Miller."

He shook his head. Mr. Beiler had said the same, but Zach didn't know how to reconcile that. Growing up, his uncle had never done a favor for a neighbor or friend without expecting something in return. Zach's high school friends had been more than happy to loan him money if they were out and Zach wanted to order a hamburger. But they'd always expected to be repaid.

Grace's eyes were flashing. "We give to you because God has blessed us. It would be selfish to hoard God's blessings."

"But I haven't done anything to deserve your kindness—the opposite, in fact."

Her gaze softened. "You don't have to deserve it. Just accept it."

He shrugged helplessly. "I'll...try."

She smiled, and because he was too close and looking right at her, he was caught, like one magnet drawn to another. His breath seized, all the air trapped inside his lungs until it became painful. He wanted to step forward and reach for her.

How would she respond if he did?

The thought jarred him and broke the pull. He quickly turned to face the stall again. Bertha had left her sleeping pups to stand and eat from the food bowl and was near enough for him to reach down and pat her. He did, face burning.

Grace was perceptive. Had she read his thoughts on his face? He would never act on the impulse. Would never do anything to jeopardize their tentative friendship.

She cleared her throat, and he heard the swish of her skirt, but she didn't leave.

"Are you still looking for your *onkle*?" she asked.

He nodded and was thankful for something to talk about. "There are too many Paul Robertses in this county. I'm planning to bike to the library and print off another list of names and phone numbers to try." He'd started with the smaller towns nearby, remembering that his uncle had complained of disliking the big city. But none of the Paul Robertses he'd spoken to on the phone had been his uncle, and every time he crossed out a name from his list, disappointment swelled.

He sighed. "Maybe he moved out of state. Maybe I should stop looking. It isn't as if I need a place to stay anymore."

She made a soft noise of disagreement. "It must be hard not to know what happened to him. Are you worried for him?"

"Kind of." Uncle Paul had had the occasional bout of bad health, but Zach had checked the county records, and there was no death certificate. His uncle had just…left.

"I need to return some books to the library. Maybe I could come with you and help."

He glanced at her in surprise. "You would?"

Was she blushing? Color filled her cheeks, but she was probably just cold. "It might lighten your burden to have a friend along."

A friend. Of course. But Zach wanted it so badly that he couldn't say no. "Thank you."

A few minutes later, he was wheeling his bike toward where she stood with hers, near the front porch of the big house. She was bundled in a dark coat and scarf and gloves.

"Violet just reminded me about *Daed*'s Christmas supper next week. You're coming, aren't you?"

He'd forgotten about it. Or maybe he'd put it out of his mind. She must've seen his grimace, because her expression changed into a stubborn look he'd seen her use on her brothers. "You have to come. All of *Daed*'s employees and their families will be here."

Amos had told Zach all about the event. The Beilers would open their home to host a huge meal and potluck gathering to celebrate the Christmas season. He'd been grateful for his growing friendship with Amos, but most of Mr. Beiler's other workers still kept their distance from Zach. It might be uncomfortable.

"I would hate to disappoint your *daed*," he said. Which wasn't really an answer at all.

She leveled a look on him that told him she'd seen right through him.

He began pushing his bike toward the street, and she did the same, falling into step beside him.

"If I do attend," he said, "I'll need to bring

something. I don't want to be the only one to show up without a food contribution."

"The bakery has a lot of choices."

He made a *pssht* sound. "And listen to Amos tease me all night?"

She laughed. "True. What are you thinking of making, then?"

"I don't know how to cook anything," he admitted. "But I liked your *mamm*'s apple dumplings last week."

"I could teach you."

He glanced at her. He hadn't meant to finagle an invitation out of her. His heart pounded at the idea of spending more time with her.

"If you wrote down the recipe, I'm sure I could fumble through."

She wrinkled her nose.

"No?" he asked.

"For one thing, the recipe is up here." She tapped her temple.

"Ah." He hadn't thought about that. "If you aren't tired of helping me after today…and if you're sure. That would be nice." Spending time with Grace in the kitchen? It would be both pleasure and torture.

*"Goot,"* she said.

She kicked one leg over her bicycle. "I'll race you to the stop sign."

\* \* \*

Grace had never laughed so much on a bicycle before.

After she'd barely beat him to the stop sign, he'd begun clowning around. Riding with both feet off the pedals. Zigzagging around her in slow circles. Making his bike hop like a bunny, with both wheels off the ground for a short time.

When she'd dared ride for a few yards with no hands, he'd exclaimed in appreciation. And then her front tire had hit a loose piece of gravel and wobbled so that she'd had to quickly grab the handlebars before she took a tumble.

Zach's hearty laugh was worth any embarrassment.

By the time they'd reached the library, her cheeks were pink and chapped and aching from smiling so much.

They went inside, and she handed her returns to the librarian behind the desk.

"Isaiah asked me to bring him a couple of books. The children's section is upstairs." She pointed to the staircase off to one side of the tiled entrance. The library had once been a stately house, converted long ago to this community building. "I'll meet you at the computer bank in a few minutes?"

He nodded. The library boasted three computers for public use, and the desks for those were tucked off to one side of the ground floor.

Upstairs, she found Isaiah's books and browsed the new magazines, looking for the new issue of the birding magazine *Daed* enjoyed. It wasn't out yet.

Two novels called to her from an endcap, and she added them to the growing stack in her arms.

She was returning to the ground floor, half-way down the staircase, when she caught sight of Zach talking with a man she didn't recognize.

She faltered and paused.

Zach's back was to her. The man with him was an *Englisher*, dressed in a hooded sweat-shirt and jeans that were ripped at the knee. He must have been about Zach's age, though his hair was shaved close to his head.

She tried not to judge others on their appearance. She had been gawked at many times by tourists who thought the Amish way of life and dress were strange or something to be pointed at. She didn't like it. So she tried not to do it to others.

But there was something about this man—a hard light in his eyes or the lines on his face—that frightened her a little.

This was not someone she would have approached on the street. Who was he? Why was Zach talking to him?

Zach shook his head, cutting off whatever the other man was saying. He glanced around but didn't see Grace where she stood near the top of the staircase. Zach shifted his feet like he was agitated, and she couldn't help but wonder why.

*Zach Miller isn't what he seems.* Sarah's hard words from weeks ago slithered through Grace's brain like a spiteful serpent.

Grace slipped back upstairs, cocooning herself in a tiny nook behind a bookshelf filled with baby books. Her heart was pounding, and she chided herself for overreacting.

Zach could talk to whomever he wanted. Just because he was talking with an *Englisher* didn't mean he was doing anything untoward. But Grace hadn't liked the look of that man, and Zach's agitation bothered her.

She was being silly, letting Sarah's suspicion and dislike of Zach carry her away. She wasn't Zach's keeper. He didn't need one.

With a determined straightening of her shoulders, she went downstairs. Zach was alone, sitting at one of the computers. She joined him, setting Isaiah's books on the desk in between the two keyboards.

He looked up at her with a small smile. "You

like to read, huh?" He nodded to the stack of books.

"I love to read." Tension coiled in her belly. She tried to make her words breezy and casual. "I thought I heard you talking with someone."

His smile disappeared. "An old friend saw me come inside from the street and wanted to say hi." But as he explained, his eyes shifted slightly away, as if perhaps he wasn't telling the whole truth.

Her stomach did a slow flip.

But she firmed her lips. Zach had given her no reason to believe he was up to no good. *Daed* wouldn't have let him stay if he thought Zach would get into trouble. If Zach didn't want to tell her what his conversation had been about, that was his right.

But even as they searched the internet for more Paul Robertses, her curiosity remained.

## Chapter Ten

Later that week, Zach entered the back door of the *daadi haus* after work. He removed his coat and hat and hung them on a hook near the door. He ran one hand through his hair, grateful that these few weeks without the prison's clippers had given his hair a chance to grow.

He used one hand to rub the tension gathered at the back of his neck.

He'd been unsettled since Saturday morning, when his old friend Christopher Evans had followed him into the library.

He hadn't seen Christopher since the day he'd been arrested. Being face-to-face with his old friend had been like looking into a mirror of the Zach that might've been if he hadn't returned to his faith.

Christopher wore a hoodie and jeans. Beneath the clothes, Zach could see how skinny he was.

He smelled like he hadn't had a shower in two days. And based on how he squinted against the overhead lights, Zach suspected he might be hungover.

After Zach had gently rebuffed Christopher's invitation to hang out sometime, the other man's gaze had grown quizzical.

"C'mon, man. Several of the old gang still live in town. I'll send a couple of messages. It'll be like old times."

*Old times.*

Zach didn't want to go back to those days. Some things in his life might be painful. Like the way Sarah still glared at him when their paths crossed. Or the guilt that woke him up in the dark part of night and kept him from sleeping.

But instead of turning to alcohol to numb him, he clung to God's Word.

He'd tried to explain it to Christopher, but his former friend had blown him off when it was clear Zach wasn't up for a party.

Zach had been relieved to be rid of him before Grace had returned with her books. He didn't know whether Grace would've been understanding about the conversation. It was easier not to have to explain.

But the encounter had been bugging him all week.

"I'm in here, watering the violets." Grace's

sweet voice rang out through the living room doorway. "Give me another few minutes, and I'll be ready for your cooking lesson."

He moved to stand in the doorway, propping one shoulder against the jamb as he watched her. She moved from plant to plant, looking here, touching a fuzzy leaf there. She had a tiny watering can in her hand, and occasionally she dripped some water onto one of the pots.

"They are overflowing their shelves," he commented.

She sent him a chagrined smile. "I have a big order going out this weekend. It will free up some space."

"Your seedlings are going to need to be transplanted into larger pots soon, aren't they?"

She glanced at him, her surprise evident.

He felt a blush warm his neck and ears. "I was just looking at them. I didn't touch them." He would never admit how many times he'd loitered over the plants, imagining Grace caring for them the way she was right now.

"I don't mind." There came her warm smile. "You can look all you like."

Her words hung between them. His gaze took her in hungrily. He'd noticed her hands when she'd been typing on the computer keyboard at the library. They were slender and graceful. Somehow they were also strong enough to do daily chores for her family and to care for her plants.

She stepped back, her attention on the shelves and plants. "Too many more orders and I'll have to start turning them away. Unless I can find somewhere else to grow them."

Pleasure suffused him. He'd started building a Christmas gift for Grace—with her father's permission—and when he was done, it would solve her space problem.

Grace and her family had explained that their Christmas was focused more on family and relationships than on exchanging gifts. But he had wanted to do something tangible for Grace. Right now, he was keeping the parts of the gift that were finished at Mr. Beiler's shop. He would be ready to start assembling it soon and would have it completed before Christmas.

Grace seemed to shake herself from whatever musings she had been lost in, as she stared at her flowers. She replaced the watering can on a plastic-covered shelf in the corner of the room and turned to him with brows raised. "Are you ready to bake? Let me wash up."

They met in the kitchen. Last night, he'd unloaded the supplies he'd picked up from the grocery. Flour and baking powder and salt. Apples and sweet milk.

Somehow, Grace was going to help him turn this into dumplings.

Nerves tangled in his stomach, and he didn't know whether they were from the desire to please his boss and coworkers or from being in such close proximity to Grace.

She instructed him to set out all the ingredients on the counter. She moved around him, fishing in different drawers and beneath the cabinets, adding a peeler, a mixing bowl, measuring spoons and cups, and a tool with a cylindrical end that he didn't have a name for.

She held up the peeler. "Step one. Peel the apples."

He wasn't sure what he'd expected, but she seemed determined that he perform each task on his own.

She let him fumble with the apples, his hands too large to handle the delicate peeler. By the time he'd peeled six apples, he'd nicked his knuckle once and was sticky. The small cut stung from the acidic juice.

"*Goot* job."

He sent her a skeptical look that made her lips twitch.

"For a beginner?" he asked.

She nodded, a smile blooming across her lips. He didn't even mind that she found him amusing.

She showed him how to use the apple corer—

the tool he hadn't known. That one wasn't so difficult.

Next, she instructed him on mixing the dough and rolling it out on the counter. He was beginning to feel a stirring of confidence. Maybe this wasn't so hard.

But when it was time to wrap the peeled and cored apples in small squares of the dough, his first attempt looked like a mangled mess.

He frowned at the funky-looking dough ball.

But Grace was all smiles and encouragement. "Try again. You'll get the hang of it."

His second try was worse than the first.

"Stop being so hard on yourself," she chided him. She leaned against the opposite side of the counter, watching him.

He put a third apple onto a third square. This time, the dough wouldn't stick and fell away from the apple completely. He gripped the countertop. "I can't see how I'm doing it wrong. My hands are too big, I think."

His hopes for impressing Mr. Beiler and Amos with his dessert were gone. Right now he would settle for something edible.

Grace's lips twitched, as if she was having a hard time holding in a giggle.

The heat of his embarrassment faded. She didn't seem to mind that he was awful at this.

He'd make a fool of himself all day long just to see her smile.

He mock-glared at her but then couldn't help a reluctant laugh. "I'm terrible."

Her laughter pealed, and just the sound of it made his spirits lift. "You're not terrible."

For all his determination to do this himself, he was going to have to buy something at the bakery. He fisted his hands on the counter.

"Maybe I can show you instead of explaining it." She rounded the countertop and sidled in close. So close that her shoulder brushed his bicep.

He held his breath.

She pointed at the dumpling he'd started assembling. When he hesitated, she reached out and rested each of her hands over the top of his.

The unexpected touch made him freeze. Her fingers were warm and dry from the flour. His heartbeat rushed in his ears.

She froze, too. "I—I didn't think." She lifted her hands away, holding them in the air in front of her. "I know you don't like to be touched."

That's what she thought?

His body was still frozen in the moment when she had touched him, and it took a deep breath to bring him back to his senses.

"I don't dislike it," he said, his voice low. "Sometimes it's a surprise. The prison guards didn't touch us much, but when they did it wasn't gentle." He left it at that. "And my uncle was never one for hugs or anything like that."

He couldn't ever remember Paul riffling his hair, like he saw Isaiah and Elijah's older sisters do frequently. The two brothers might tussle and wrestle with each other, but he'd also seen Elijah sling his arm over Isaiah's shoulder as they'd walked out to the barn. And Grace was used to giving a gentle touch on an arm or a squeeze of someone's hand. He'd watched her enough that he'd seen it over and over again.

Touch was one of the reasons he had fallen hard for Tiffany back in high school. He had been so starved for affection that he'd taken everything she had offered him, even though he had known better.

He blinked away those thoughts. Grace was still standing close and looking at him with compassion-filled eyes.

He didn't want her to make a big deal out of it. And as if she'd somehow sensed his wishes, she looked back down at the waiting dumpling.

"If you're sure you don't mind, then I'll just…" She took his hands again, and this time he was ready for her touch. At least he thought he was, but blood was pounding in his ears again. He could barely hear her instructions as she manipulated his fingers and the dough.

With her fingers guiding him, he could feel exactly how to pinch the dough together, and when she lifted their hands away, the resulting dumpling was miles above his terrible ones. He'd take it.

"Try again."

He did, and with his new knowledge, this one turned out slightly better.

"Now we bake them?" he asked.

She oversaw him putting the dumplings on a baking sheet and into the oven.

When he straightened, she was watching him with a smile tugging at her lips.

"What?"

Her smile bloomed. "You have a little flour…"

She pointed to the side of her nose, and he used his wrist, the only part of his hand that wasn't covered in flour, to attempt to wipe it off.

He looked at her with his brows raised.

She shook her head. "Let me."

It was natural to turn toward her slightly.

She raised up on her tiptoes and reached out. The brush of her fingers on his nose and then his cheek was almost as light as a feather. Sensation bloomed from the place she had touched, heating his face and lighting up everything inside him.

Looking down at her like this, with a smile playing on her lips, and her eyes shining up at him, he wanted so badly to place his hands on her hips. To draw her slightly closer…

He threw himself out of those thoughts. He turned away so quickly that she had to step back or be knocked over.

He had to stop thinking about her like that. Stop wanting more. Grace was his friend. And that had to be enough.

He wasn't worthy of her. How could he be? He was responsible for Thomas's death.

It had been too much to bear for Tiffany. After his arrest, she had walked away after a tense two-minute phone call where she'd broken up with him. He'd thought they were tight. She knew more about him than anyone else. They'd still been in high school, but he'd been sure she was the one.

His tumbling thoughts made the silent moment awkward.

Grace looked down, wiping her hands on her apron.

Anxious now, he gestured toward the mess he'd made of the counter. "I'll clean up."

"I can help."

"No!" He hadn't meant to refuse so forcefully. "I mean, no, thank you. You've helped enough already."

She shifted her feet. "I guess… I'll go, then."

He couldn't help glancing at her. She was

looking at him with a question in her eyes, but he didn't know what the question was, and he couldn't imagine she wanted to stay for the entire time until the dumplings were done baking.

"That's probably a *goot* idea."

But as she turned for the door, he couldn't keep from calling out her name.

She looked back with one hand on the open door.

"*Danke*. For everything."

And then she was gone.

## Chapter Eleven

The house was full to bursting with friends.

Grace watched her *daed*'s employees and their families enjoy themselves at the gathering. Every chair around the dining table was full, and *Mamm* had set up two folding tables in the living room. Other friends stood in small groups, holding their plates and chatting.

The house was decorated for the season, with boughs of evergreen trimmed with red ribbon on the mantel and ornamenting the staircase railing. Grace wore a deep green dress.

Everyone seemed to be filled with cheer befitting the Christmas season. She was the only one filled with nervous tension.

Before he'd prayed for the meal, *Daed* had announced that the shop had had a successful year and he already had several big jobs lined up for the new year. Things were good.

And then he'd called on Zach to pray for the food.

Zach had been up for the challenge, and afterward, Grace had noticed several of the workers from *Daed*'s shop come up and shake Zach's hand. From across the room, Sarah had watched Zach with narrowed eyes. Grace had worried that her sister might make a public scene, but Sarah had whirled and disappeared into the crowd.

Grace had been unsettled since she'd left Zach to clean up his mess after the apple dumpling–making lesson. She'd only meant to help him get the flour off his face, but then she'd thought she had seen… Well, she'd thought that maybe he was going to lean in and kiss her.

Would she have turned away if he had?

She didn't know.

When she'd come inside the big house, Sarah had been standing at the kitchen window. If she'd stood there long enough, she would've seen Grace leave the *daadi haus*. That wasn't unusual. Sarah knew that Grace had to care for her violets.

But when Sarah had looked at Grace…somehow, she knew that Grace had been with Zach. Or maybe Grace's guilt showed in her expression. Sarah's eyes had sparkled with tears.

When Grace had feared she would receive a

tongue lashing from her sister, Sarah had simply turned and gone to her room.

Grace had tried to engage her sister in conversation in the days after, but Sarah barely responded. She was withdrawn and quiet. And her silence hurt. Grace hated to lose the closeness she and Sarah had always shared. Especially when she hadn't done anything wrong.

In contrast to Grace's tension, Zach seemed more settled tonight. As she served glasses of lemonade and punch, she covertly watched him interact with his coworkers from *Daed*'s shop. He seemed…lighter, somehow.

It was his smile. Until now, she had never seen it come so easily.

Especially when she'd caught him looking in her direction. She couldn't help blushing every time their eyes connected. He looked so handsome tonight, with his hair combed neatly and his shirt freshly pressed.

The line for folks getting drinks trickled to the occasional straggler, and Grace took her chance to make herself a plate from the goodness overflowing the long kitchen island.

When she moved back into the dining room, she caught sight of Amos through a break in the crowd. He waved her over. It wasn't until she'd nearly reached him that she saw he was standing with Zach. Grace couldn't help a surreptitious glance around. Sarah was nowhere in sight.

Besides, she was only conversing with her cousin and a friend. Nothing wrong with that.

"Hallo, Amos. Zach."

"Hallo." Zach's eyes brimmed with warmth.

"I need your help," Amos said in lieu of a greeting.

"With what?" She took a bite of creamy mashed potatoes, the food melting in her mouth. She'd been helping *Mamm* in the kitchen all day, breathing in the delicious aromas of everything they were cooking, but *Mamm* had refused to let her taste.

"He's been sending love notes to someone, and he's messed it up," Zach offered.

Amos winced.

She bounced on her toes. This was news to her. "Oh! Who is it?"

Zach shook his head. "He won't tell me."

If she wasn't mistaken, Amos was blushing. Color crept up his neck and into his cheeks. "I only sent the first note to sort of feel her out… but then she wrote me back—at least I thought it was her—and I kept writing, and…"

"There've been numerous letters exchanged," Zach said helpfully.

Amos looked miserable. "And yesterday I

found out that she wasn't writing me back at all—it was her sister."

Oh dear. Poor Amos. She couldn't help asking again, "Who is it?"

"I don't want to say. It's a disaster." Amos rubbed one hand over his face.

"How can I help you if I don't know who it is?"

He groaned. "I don't know. I just want the whole thing to go away."

She patted her cousin on his forearm and then for good measure she gave Zach a raise of her eyebrows and squeezed his forearm, too. He smiled, and she felt it all the way to her toes.

"Please, let's talk about something else," Amos said. "Have you had an update from *Aendi* Martha?"

"*Mamm* and Violet visited yesterday, and she was sitting up in her chair. Verity says she's improving, though she still gets fatigued easily."

Amos frowned. "Will *Aendi* Martha be able to come for Christmas lunch?"

*Mamm*'s extended family usually gathered for a meal on Christmas Day at Esther and Will's. But Grace didn't know whether Martha would be up to attending the event, and she said as much. She missed having her sister at home. Verity was soft-spoken and shy, but things weren't the same without her around.

A comfortable silence fell. Voices rose and fell as friends chatted. Isaiah ran through the room, almost bumping into Jacob Troyer. One of his young friends chased him. Grace thought about going after them before her brother could cause an accident, but the boys ran upstairs, so she left them to their fun.

She caught sight of one of the Glick boys—nearly grown now—taking a bite of a familiar dessert.

"Your dumplings must be a success," she told Zach. "There weren't any left by the time I saw your serving pan."

Amos raised his brows. "You baked? I think I had one of those. It was *goot*."

Zach smiled bashfully. "Grace taught me how to make them."

She grinned at him. "How long did it take you to peel all those apples?" She'd seen the mound of dumplings that had been in the pan.

He narrowed his eyes playfully. "I refuse to admit it."

"Are you going to start bringing desserts to the shop?" Amos asked. He smacked his lips. "Bring enough to share."

"I wasn't planning on it." Zach rolled his eyes as he said the words. "Mastering a few cooking skills will help when I have to move on from the

Beilers' *daadi haus*. I'll be sick of dumplings, but I won't starve."

Amos chuckled, but Grace felt a stirring of unease. She knew Zach didn't plan to stay forever, but his words made it sound as if he would be moving on soon. She wasn't sure what to think about his statement, and her smile faltered.

Amos didn't seem to notice anything amiss. "Grace, did your *daed* find out anything about the mess left at the shop?"

Zach expressed the same curiosity she felt. "What mess?"

Amos looked between them. "You don't know? Two days ago, someone must've had a party behind the building. Out back, near where we park our bikes. They left a bunch of beer cans behind." He gestured at Zach with his lemonade glass. "We found it that morning you came in late."

Amos glanced across the room and didn't see the way Zach's face suddenly went pale, but Grace noticed.

"Why didn't *Daed* mention it to us?" He hadn't breathed a word to his family.

Amos shrugged. "*Onkle* Iddo said he wanted to ask a few men if they'd seen anything. But if it happened at night, after we closed up the shop…"

All her *daed*'s workers would be home eating supper with their families. The shop was on a lane with a furniture store and a quilting shop. Both of them closed around suppertime. With no residences close by, who would've seen anything at all?

Amos must've seen her concern. "Don't worry. *Onkle* Iddo looked the shop over. No one tried to break in. It was probably some kids out having fun."

Zach blanched. He'd been silent, listening to Amos. Now his eyes scanned the room. His expression had lost the openness and lightness he'd worn earlier when he'd teased Amos.

"I need to find your *daed*," he said.

"Zach, wait. You can talk to *Daed* later—"

But he'd already taken his leave, striding across the room to deposit his empty plate in the kitchen.

Amos looked at her, confused. "What happened?"

She didn't know. Amos had been talking about the vandalism at *Daed*'s shop, and Zach had sounded so serious. Maybe even stricken. What was he worried about?

She watched him disappear through the dining room doorway. His shoulders reflected a tension that had been completely absent before Amos's offhand comment.

Sarah forgotten, Grace realized she wanted—

needed—to see Zach's easy smile return. She'd been working on a Christmas surprise. Maybe tonight was the night to give it to him.

After the party, she would do just that.

Zach felt as if he was going to be sick.

He moved through the crowd, for the first time feeling overwhelmed at the press of bodies. He'd grown used to being around people like this. He'd thought his memories from prison were fading, but right now the same anxiety tightened his belly.

Had it gotten warmer in here? Or was he simply overheating?

Up until now, he'd been having a good time at the party. His coworkers had introduced him to their wives and small children. Amos had been full of stories of big Christmases shared with his huge extended family. Zach couldn't remember having experienced a Christmas like that, full of family and laughter and warmth.

When Grace had joined them and smiled at him, he'd felt on top of the world. As if he *could* be accepted into the Walnut Cove community.

And then Amos's words, innocently spoken, had drenched Zach's enjoyment in icy water. Grace hadn't connected the dots, but that didn't mean someone else wouldn't. Beer cans and probably cigarette butts? The mess that Amos described was eerily similar to what he and his friends would leave behind on nights when they got together drinking.

Even now his insides felt frozen, the same way they had on the night he'd sat in the back of a cop car, watching flashing blue and red lights illuminate the emergency workers as they'd tried to save a man's life.

He hadn't touched alcohol since he had been sent to prison, but what if Mr. Beiler suspected Zach had been a part of what had happened?

He found Mr. Beiler near the front door, saying goodbye to Ezekial Glick and his obviously pregnant wife. The couple excused themselves, and Mr. Beiler turned to Zach.

"Something troubling you?" the older man asked.

Zach looked around at the faces of the men he worked with every day. They were smiling and chatting, unaware that anything might be wrong. He felt a desperate, immediate desire that none of them overhear his conversation with Mr. Beiler.

"Do you mind if we step outside?"

Mr. Beiler followed him out the front door, and they stood on the stoop together, both shivering in their shirtsleeves.

Zach struggled for words.

And Mr. Beiler was no help. It was a running

joke in the Beiler family, and even Zach had
noticed that the head of the family was never
quick to speak. Zach knew he could learn a lesson from that. But right now he would give anything for Mr. Beiler to offer him an opening.

There was nothing for it but to jump right in.
"Amos mentioned that someone had left a bunch
of beer cans outside the shop."

Mr. Beiler's steady gaze never wavered.

The sick feeling in Zach's stomach intensified. He fisted his hands at his sides. "I want you
to know that I don't do that anymore. I don't."

Mr. Beiler waited a bit, as if he expected Zach
to say something more. When Zach didn't, he
nodded slowly. *"Goot."*

*Goot?* That was all?

Zach stared at the man in disbelief. "Don't
you want me to tell you where I was on the night
the beer cans showed up?"

Mr. Beiler's eyes were plenty sharp. "Am I a
policeman to ask that? Besides, I know where
you were. You were here, at my table, helping
Isaiah with his math homework."

Zach didn't know whether he should feel
relieved or concerned that Mr. Beiler already
knew his alibi. Was Mr. Beiler keeping tabs on
him? Or was it much simpler than that?

The older man's gaze was across the yard,

focused on the *daadi haus.* "You've been with us for several weeks now."

Zach's stomach plummeted. Mr. Beiler was going to ask him to leave. Zach's presence had caused trouble enough. Sarah was still cold to him. And now this. He braced himself for it.

But the words Zach expected to hear didn't come. Instead Mr. Beiler said, "You're a *goot* worker. I'd like to keep you on at the shop permanently."

Zach was floored. It took him a moment too long to process the unexpected words. He blinked and he couldn't be sure, but it seemed that Mr. Beiler had a twinkle in his eyes, as if he might be smiling at Zach's expense.

"You want to stay in Walnut Cove, *jah?*"

Zach nodded.

"Then you need a permanent job. To save up for a house of your own, hmm?"

Zach had tried not to think about his future. For so long, his only plan had been to get released and find his uncle.

But that hadn't happened, and he'd ended up here, under Mr. Beiler's wing.

"Can I pray about it?"

It was the right answer, because Mr. Beiler smiled and extended his hand for Zach to shake.

Before they could go inside and rejoin the party, a car rolled into the driveway, its headlights flashing across them. The sight was so unusual among the buggies and bicycles that Zach couldn't process it for a moment.

He squinted against the bright lights as the car pulled to a stop. If Bertha hadn't been locked in the barn with her pups, she would've barked an alert.

The driver's side door opened. "Is that you, Zach?"

Zach was dumbfounded to hear the familiar voice. Tiffany. His former girlfriend.

He looked to Mr. Beiler and then back at the woman standing beside her beat-up car. He'd just told his boss and friend that he didn't associate with his old friends. And Tiffany showed up out of the blue.

Why was she here?

"I don't—" He looked to Mr. Beiler, stunned and uncertain. "That's my old girlfriend. I haven't seen her in years."

The older man ducked inside and returned immediately with Zach's coat. "You should see what she wants."

Zach took the coat and shrugged into it. He went down the steps, meeting Tiffany in front of her car. The engine ticked as it cooled. She'd left the headlights on, but now that they shined on the house and not in his eyes, he got a closer look at her.

She looked so much different than he remembered. Older. Her hair was dark brown and past her shoulders. When he'd dated her, she'd had it dyed with blond streaks. Back then, she had worn heavy makeup. Now her face was a pale smudge against the darkness.

"What are you doing here?" he asked. "How did you find me?"

She stared at him so long and hard that he grew uncomfortable. "I heard you were back in town. I ran into Christopher, and he said he'd seen you at the…library? Or something." She said the words as if she didn't believe it.

And yeah, he wouldn't have been caught dead in the library when he'd been a stupid teenager.

"I saw him." His former friend had smelled just the way Zach remembered, clearly up to his old ways. He'd invited Zach to come party at the place he was renting, but Zach had turned him down flat.

"Christopher said you were all religious now, but I didn't want to believe him."

She was still staring at him. He stared back, remembering how he'd once felt about her. But it had been four years. There was nothing there now. She'd never visited him in prison. There'd only been that breakup phone call. Whatever feelings he'd had for her were gone.

"Are you…one of them now?"

He looked back at the house. Through the big living room window, he could see the outline of a couple. A man in a white shirt and suspenders and a woman in a blue dress. Grace was wearing a dress of deep green that had made her glow. Grace wasn't in the window, but she was inside. And that's where he wanted to be.

He looked back at Tiffany. "I hope so."

Her lips parted as if she wanted to say more. There was something in her expression, an uncertainty or disappointment, he didn't know which.

"Was there a reason you needed to talk to me?" he asked, more than ready to go back to the gathering. If Tiffany wanted to ask him to party, he'd shut her down just like he'd done to Christopher.

She stared at him a moment longer, then shook her head and got in the car.

He was left questioning why she'd shown up. There had to be a reason.

But when he ducked back inside the warmth of the Beilers' house, he caught sight of Grace in that green dress and forgot all about Tiffany.

## Chapter Twelve

Zach was carting folding chairs down to the basement as the Beilers cleaned up after the party. When he returned upstairs after the last trip, Grace's *mamm* was ushering Isaiah and Elijah upstairs. Sarah and Violet had disappeared. Mr. Beiler was sitting at the dining table with a cup of *kaffee* and his Bible open.

And Grace was waiting in the front room with Zach's coat. Time to go.

He said good-night to his boss and strode toward her. As he neared, he saw she was wearing her coat, too.

"Will you walk down to the barn with me?" she asked.

His stomach did a slow flip. Had she somehow figured out his Christmas surprise? He nodded.

Seeing Tiffany again had given him closure

on the relationship that hadn't lasted past his indictment. He felt nothing for her.

In contrast, just stepping out of the house and falling into stride beside Grace—they weren't even touching—had his pulse racing.

Their boots crunched through the frosty winter grass. A slender moon rose over the horizon, and it limned her skin with silver.

One glance from her and he could fall into her eyes. Heat flushed his face, and he forced his gaze away, forced himself to look at the barn. "Do you need me to cart some pots to the *daadi haus*?"

"No." She smiled a soft smile. "There's a surprise for you out here."

"A surprise?" For him? "Really?"

"*Jah*, really." She tilted her head toward him. "You seem shocked. More than a little surprise like this deserves."

He *was* shocked. "It's been a long time since anyone has made a surprise for me. Probably my *mamm* when I was a kid was the last one." His teachers in middle school and high school had been too busy, with heavy workloads, to notice a lonely kid like him.

Grace reached the barn door first and turned so that she partially blocked his way. He could've moved away, but found he didn't want to look away from her compassionate gaze.

"I'm sorry, Zach."

He stuffed his hands into his coat pockets. "It wasn't your fault." It wasn't anybody's fault, really, that he'd been stuck with an uncle who didn't want the burden of raising a kid.

"Things have been so much better for me since coming back here." And Grace was a part of all of it. Because of Grace, he'd formed friendships, had a job, experienced beauty. Every time he saw that plant in his bedroom window, it made him think of her. He was so grateful for her that he couldn't form words. He hoped she knew.

The silence between them seemed to swell with anticipation.

Since the night she'd helped him bake and he'd almost given in to the impulse to kiss her, he couldn't get Amos's suggestion out of his head—he should invite Grace to walk home with him from the next singing.

But Grace was popular. What if…? What if there was someone special?

The thought made his stomach roil. There was only one way to find out.

"I have been wondering," he started haltingly, "if there's anyone—"

Her curious gaze unmanned him, and he broke off. He cleared his throat. Started over. "You have given me good advice since the day

I arrived in Walnut Cove. Like with the dumplings." Only this was so much more.

She smiled. "Of course."

He swallowed hard. "I was thinking of asking—someone—" he stumbled over the words "—if she would walk home with me from the next singing."

Grace's expression lost none of its warmth.

"Whoever she is, she would be a fool to say no." She glanced down shyly. He couldn't be sure in the moonlight, but he thought she might be blushing. "*Daed* thinks very highly of you. And so do I." She added the last in a whisper.

That was the confirmation that he had been waiting for, softly uttered with Grace's humble spirit.

He was going to do this. "It's you, Grace. The one that I want to ask. Would you let me walk you home from the singing?"

She glanced away, her eyes going over his shoulder into the darkness. Her gaze was soft and unfocused, and she bit her lip as if she might be conflicted.

He heard a ringing in his ears.

She was going to say *no*.

But when she looked up, her eyes were soft and determined. She nodded, and he felt a weight lift from his shoulders. *Yes.*

Happiness burst forth in a grin he couldn't

contain, and her lips spread in a responding smile.

"You should do that more often. Smile," she added.

"You've given me much to be happy about tonight."

"Don't forget about your surprise."

That's right. They hadn't even made it into the barn.

She pushed open the door and motioned him to follow her inside. Right now he would follow her wherever she wanted to go.

She led him to Bertha's stall, where the puppies were awake and playful. The five little bodies had more than doubled their size and were roly little fluff balls. Grace stepped close to the blocked-off area that kept them safe inside and squatted down, making kissing noises.

The puppies bounced and tumbled their way to her, giving happy yips.

One of the puppies had a cheerful red ribbon tied around its neck in a bow. That was the one that Grace scooped up and held in her arms. The other puppies attacked her feet, but she ignored them, instead carefully turning to Zach. She was a picture, glowing with beauty from within and holding the black-and-white pup just below her chin. Zach never wanted to forget this moment.

"I talked to *Daed* and the boys, and we all decided that you must have one of Bertha's puppies. It's our Christmas gift to you."

Maybe he should've guessed her intent by the puppy's festive ribbon, but it took a moment for her words to sink in. When they did, he shook his head. "What?"

She took one careful step closer, looking down to make sure the puppies had moved away. They'd raced off into a corner, now chasing a loose piece of hay. She reached out, and there was nothing for it but for him to accept the pup from her extended hands. Its body was warm and wiggly, and the first thing it did was lick his chin.

Prickly heat poked the back of his throat, and he swallowed to try and clear it.

The pup nibbled the collar of his coat and then curled into a ball against the warmth of Zach's chest. He shifted it in his hands. A little girl, a bundle of love like her mother.

He swallowed hard. "Grace, I can't. It's too much."

She'd remembered the one time he'd mentioned that he'd always wanted a dog and had never been allowed. She said she'd spoken to her *daed*, but she alone would've known how much this meant to him.

"No arguments," she said firmly. "It's already decided."

He bowed his head, closed his eyes. Could he do this? Accept this gift? The puppy's chest rose and fell with each tiny breath. *Yes.*

He opened his eyes. "Thank you, Grace."

"Now she just needs a name."

He rubbed his cheek against the softness of the puppy's head. "That will take some thinking."

Zach knew the pup would need to stay with her mother for several more weeks before she was ready to be weaned. But after tonight's talk with Mr. Beiler and now this, he knew with certainty that Walnut Cove was where he wanted to have the next chapter of his life written.

He wanted so much more than that, but he didn't dare think those thoughts. Not with the showers of blessings he'd already experienced tonight.

His heart was overflowing, and suddenly, it was imperative that he give Grace her gift tonight, as well. It wouldn't be a complete gift, but he needed her to see it.

Grace could almost feel Zach's nervousness in the air between them as he ushered her back outside and around the side of the barn.

He wasn't the only one who was nervous.

She'd agreed to walk home with him, even though she knew it might hurt Sarah. What kind of sister was she? But Zach had been so earnest, and…

She wanted to go with him. She wanted to spend more time with him. She would have to speak with Sarah about it before Sunday.

Right now she was distracted by his surprise.

He'd spent several minutes loving on his new puppy before he'd tucked her back in with Bertha and her brothers and sisters. When he'd told Grace he had something to show her, her curiosity was piqued.

Now he had one hand tucked in his coat pocket. The other held the flashlight. "It isn't finished yet, so don't expect much."

She was shivering from both the cold and anticipation. She hadn't expected him to have a surprise of his own.

"Also, I think I measured wrong on one side, so I may have to fix a couple of boards—"

When he hesitated at the corner of the barn, she drew even with him.

"Zach. I'm sure it's perfectly lovely. Whatever it is." Her imagination was going wild. What would he be doing out behind the barn?

She saw the vulnerability in his expression. He wanted to please her. That thought filled her with warmth, making her forget for a moment the chilly night air. She slipped her arm through his elbow and leaned into his side. "Show me."

He stepped forward, and she moved with him around the corner. His flashlight illuminated the bare frame of what appeared to be…a lean-to? The small addition to the barn was roughly the size of her bedroom and was built against the barn's southern wall.

"It's meant to be a greenhouse for you. For your flowers."

Even through the layers of both their coats, she felt the fine tremor go through his arm.

"Zach," she breathed. "It's…*wunderbaar.*"

She felt his deep inhale. "I still have to stretch the plastic for the walls. The door will be there." He pointed the beam of the flashlight at one end of the lean-to.

"It's so big! Think of how many violets I can grow. If I start selling so many, I might have to hire Elijah to help me ship them."

"He only wants to work at the shop."

She squeezed his arm. "Isaiah, then. If he can concentrate on one task for long enough."

He chuckled. He swept the flashlight across the space again. "I spent some time at the library, and I think if you put a couple of small compost bins in, you'll have plenty of heat through the winter. If that's not enough, you could add some large water drums to help retain the day's heat."

He'd done more than just built the structure. He'd researched to make sure the greenhouse would work for her needs.

He wasn't done. "I was planning to work on the interior shelves this week, after work. I was going to make them stair steps, like the ones you have now. But now that you've seen this much, maybe you want them to be a different style."

She couldn't tear her eyes from the structure, trying to picture the tiered shelves in the space.

She shook her head. "Zach, this is… This is possibly the most thoughtful thing anyone has ever done for me. How many hours have you spent on this?" The frame was well constructed, as if her *daed* had done it himself.

He shrugged, and the movement dislodged her arm. She wrapped both arms around her middle to stave off the cold. "Not that many. Amos has helped some."

She knew Zach had worked in the shop for weeks, but wasn't that mostly shaping pieces and cutting lumber? Putting together the timber framing was a skill in itself. Zach had surely spent hours getting this just right.

"It isn't just the work. You've had to start all over. You shouldn't have spent so much. The lumber alone must've cost a fortune. Won't you let me pay you back for some of it?"

He was frowning slightly now. "Your *daed* sold me the lumber at cost. And I don't want to talk about that. You said—you said that friends didn't keep track of debts. I wanted to give this to you because—"

Because what?

But he didn't finish the thought. He moved slightly away, raising his hand in agitation as if he were going to run it through his hair. He must've forgotten his hat, because he knocked it to the ground. He bent and grabbed it, using the brief seconds to hide his face from her. The flashlight bobbled, its light unsteady. He knocked his hat against his pant leg before he stuffed it back on his head. Gone was the openness he'd shown in the barn with the puppies. In its place was the carefully blank expression he'd worn in those first days.

"Zach." She hadn't meant to cause this. "I'm sorry if I offended you. This gift is… Thank you so much. This means a lot to me. That's what I should've said."

He turned his face to the side, not speaking directly to her. "When you told me about the *wunderbaar* flowers, I thought…well, that you were doing something special. Taking something broken and tending it until it grows healthy again. I wanted you to have the space you needed. I am sorry if I overstepped."

Zach shone the flashlight on the greenhouse frame again. "Maybe it is too much."

*Taking something broken and tending it until it grows healthy again.* She remembered thinking about how he was like one of her flowers. How he could flourish if he was nourished in their community.

And he'd taken to heart her simple explanation of how the plants could be propagated. He'd meant something beautiful by this gift, and her worry about his finances had taken away his joy in giving it to her. How could she make this right again?

When he turned back to her, a muscle ticked in his cheek. "Does this change your mind about walking home with me on Sunday?"

*Oh, Zach.*

"No, of course not. Why would it?"

He ducked his head. "I am not very good at this. At being a friend," he rushed on. "It was never very easy for me to make friends. Or to keep them."

Her heart pulsed a painful beat at his self-deprecating words.

He looked at the structure again, laughing a little. "It *is* too much for a gift, isn't it? It's foolish."

"It's *wunderbaar*, Zach."

At her words, he glanced up. He was trying hard to keep his expression blank, but even in the low light from the flashlight, she could see how desperately he wanted her words to be true.

Before he could question her sincerity, she gave a shiver that was only slightly exaggerated. "You'd better walk me back to the house before we both turn to blocks of ice."

He only hesitated for a moment, and she fell into step close enough beside him that it seemed natural to thread her arm through his again. This time, there was a tension between them.

"I'm grateful for your friendship," she told him.

"Right. My friendship." He murmured the words beneath his breath.

And the tension remained, though he said a polite good-night as he left her at the step. She watched him as he walked across the yard to the *daadi haus*.

Friendship. It was all she could offer him. With Sarah stubbornly set against him, she couldn't offer her heart. Even though she was beginning to want more than a simple friendship.

# *Chapter Thirteen*

Zach sat across from Grace at a long folding table in the Troyers' basement. The Sunday morning worship had been completed and a delicious lunch eaten.

Now the two of them lingered over *kaffee* as the larger group dispersed. The younger people would remain and have a time of singing and socializing.

And after that, he would be the one to walk Grace home.

It wouldn't be the same as riding home in a buggy. Amos had generously offered the use of his, but Zach had declined. He hadn't wanted his friend to forgo the gathering just so Zach could impress Grace. Besides, the Troyers' place was only a mile from the Beilers'. The walk wasn't long enough for them to get cold. Add to that the fact that Grace was probably better at driving a buggy than Zach.

"What about Apple Cider?" Grace was throwing out names for Zach's puppy. First it had been traditional dog names, none of which fit, and now she was just being silly.

"I don't like cider," he said.

"What do you mean? Everyone like cider," Grace teased him, her smile quick and bright enough to light him up from the inside out.

"I never have. Hot tea, either. But a warm cup of cocoa…" He gave an exaggerated raise of his brows to punctuate the statement.

"What about Cocoa?"

He shook his head. "It's still not the name."

She pursed her lips. "I think you're just being stubborn about this. There was nothing wrong with Daisy or Abby."

"Nothing wrong with those names. They just aren't *her* name."

She propped her chin on her hand, her eyes gone far-off as she thought.

That left him free to look at her. She wore a dress of dark red that highlighted her fair skin. Her hair was swept back and secured beneath her prayer *kapp*, like always. She blinked, and the sweep of her lashes against her cheeks made his stomach knot. She caught him looking, and her eyes crinkled in a smile. He let his eyes roam the room, as if he was looking for someone among the small groups of people standing and chatting.

Being here this evening, with Grace, was both pleasure and torture. *Friends.* That's what she wanted from him.

But that wasn't enough for him. Not anymore.

He'd realized it the same night he'd shown her the unfinished greenhouse. He'd lain awake in bed for a long time, unable to sleep for thinking about her reaction. She'd first been surprised and delighted, but then her delight had changed into something like caution.

His gesture—building her a greenhouse—wasn't one of simple friendship. It had been too big, the same way his feelings for her were growing. He could no longer contain them in a small, safe box in his heart, reserved for her. They'd grown like a wild vine, out of control.

Mr. Beiler hadn't discouraged him from building the greenhouse. Neither had Amos commented on how expensive and time-consuming the project was. Zach had thought it completely natural to want to give Grace a gift that reflected his growing admiration for her. She needed the space, after all.

He had only realized—too late—that the building and its hours of labor would be tangible proof of his feelings for her.

*I'm grateful for your friendship.* She'd been quick to put words to what she wanted from him. Friendship was more than he deserved. It was a blessing that he shouldn't take for granted.

What he needed to do was find some way to prune back his feelings for her. Find a way to contain them again in the little box marked *friendship.*

"Have you asked Isaiah for any ideas?" she asked, and it took him a moment to find the thread of conversation again. Puppy names.

He pulled a face. "His names sounded like they belonged to a cow. Dottie. Or Clarabelle."

She smiled, and he had to look away from the brightness of it.

Benjamin Troyer and his sister Miriam were taking chairs from the table's other end and arranging them in a big circle for the singing. Zach nodded so that Grace noticed them, too.

The two of them rose and started rearranging chairs, too.

"What about Checkers?" Grace suggested. She was stubbornly intent on getting him to name his puppy tonight.

He pretended to consider it. "Maybe if I named her that, Isaiah would stop beating me so badly at the game."

"Or maybe he'd be even worse."

They shared a chuckle. And she said, more

seriously, "You are *goot* for him. He looks up to you."

Zach's ears burned. He didn't know about that. "I always wished I had had a brother or sister—or a handful of them—when I was growing up."

"Even a brother like Isaiah?" She wrinkled her nose comically.

He knew she was joshing. "Even Isaiah."

"Do you hope to have a big family? When you marry?" Grace asked the question so quietly it was almost lost in the shuffle of feet and clang of chairs hitting the floor.

The old ache, the one he had experienced ever since losing his parents, panged deep inside him. "I don't know. It will be a long time before I will be settled enough to provide for a wife. I can't stay in the *daadi haus* forever."

"I think I would like a big family."

He nodded, his heart suddenly in his throat at the thought of Grace as a young mother with a baby in her arms. She would be a picture to come home to at the end of a long day. She would fill a home with warmth and peace and joy.

He shut down that line of thought before he could imagine himself being the one to walk through the door. *Friends.*

"Even if it meant having my own Elijah and Isaiah," Grace said.

He chuckled, as she'd meant him to.

He didn't want to admit it, but he was slightly jealous of Grace's brothers. The two Beiler boys had a legacy. Not only with their family, but with Mr. Beiler's company. They would grow up as apprentices, learning at their *daed*'s side. Isaiah would inherit the family home and the business when he was old enough. Their paths were laid out for them. They had a future they could count on and a strong, loving family to help make it happen.

While Zach had been granted a conditional welcome into the community and still didn't know what his future held.

The rest of the young people caught on to the rearranging of chairs, and the noise intensified. From across the room, Zach caught Sarah's pointed glare.

He fumbled the chair he'd been moving, and it toppled, landing on the floor with a loud noise. Ears hot, he bent to fix it. No one seemed to care that he'd dropped it or to have seen what he had.

He'd grown used to Sarah ignoring him completely. Her glare encompassed both him and Grace, and he had the sudden realization that Grace must be caught in the middle. Had Sarah been unkind to her because of tonight?

She hadn't mentioned it. And he should've thought to ask. But not now, in the middle of a crowd.

He kept sneaking glances at Sarah as the circle of chairs was completed. Maybe it was his imagination, but Sarah's pointed glances and whispers to the women surrounding her seemed to be directed at him.

He knew that gossip was discouraged, but that didn't mean it didn't happen. In recent weeks, he'd overheard whispered rumors of so-and-so—he couldn't even remember who now—secretly courting with Reuben Graber.

It wasn't as if he hadn't expected rumors to surround him upon his return to the community. He was surprised he hadn't noticed any until now. Not that he knew Sarah was spreading rumors, but... She glanced his way again, and her eyes sent darts.

Maybe he shouldn't have come at all. Then Sarah would have been able to have fun with her friends in peace. But if he left now, it might bring more attention to the situation, to Sarah.

Grace tugged him into the seat beside her, and he did his best to forget about Sarah and concentrate on the time together.

Songbooks were passed around the circle and when he would've taken one each for both himself and Grace, she passed one on.

"We can share," she said with a sweet smile. One that almost made him forget the guilt that plagued him.

Grace enjoyed the time of singing with Zach at her side. He had a nice baritone but sang at a low volume. She was intensely aware of his presence beside her, his arm brushing her shoulders, the tilt of his chin toward her when he looked down at the songbook in his hands.

She also couldn't help but notice Sarah's icy glare from across the room. Every time she had thought about speaking with Sarah over the past few days, she'd imagined Sarah breaking down in tears and demanding she cancel. She'd taken the coward's way out and hadn't spoken to Sarah after all.

Once the singing was over, cookies, popcorn and hot drinks were served for refreshment. Most of the courting couples were quick to depart, eager to be alone together.

She glanced to Zach. "Do you want to get something to drink? Not cider," she teased gently.

"If that's what you wish."

What she wished? She wished for him to hold her hand on the walk back home. She wished not to have a confrontation with Sarah. Her stomach twisted. "Violet and Sarah will want to stay and chat for a while."

Zach frowned, sending a quick glance across the room. What, or whom, was he looking for?

"If we want to talk with any semblance of privacy, we could sneak away now." There would be no avoiding Sarah once they arrived at home, but Grace wanted to enjoy this last bit of time with Zach. She enjoyed being at his side. Talking with him. Finding ways to make him smile.

He nodded at her suggestion, and they moved through the crowded room, saying goodbyes as they went.

"Will Verity be upset that she missed tonight?" he asked. He was close behind her as they climbed the stairs to the Troyers' first floor. "I heard one of her friends asking for her."

It had probably been Caleb. And Verity wouldn't be sorry to have missed him.

"Verity has always been shy. She would rather stay home and read than attend the singings. I think she found being sequestered at *Aendi* Martha's more of a delight than anything else."

They reached the foyer, and she headed toward the overflowing coatrack near the front door. This level of the Troyers' house was quiet and empty.

"What about you?" she asked as she reached for her coat. She found Zach's as well and handed it to him. "You've been to several social events. Would you rather be back at the *daadi haus*?"

He shrugged into the coat. "No. I've been alone long enough. Tonight's been fun." But there was a shadow behind his eyes.

"You've got something…" She reached up to his shoulder, where a piece of hay was stuck beneath the collar of his coat. She plucked the piece of straw and held it up for his examination. For once, he hadn't flinched away from her touch. "I suppose you were rolling around in the hay with the puppies?"

He shrugged self-consciously. "I guess you've never walked away from tending your plants with a smudge of dirt across your cheek."

"No. Never." She kept her eyes wide and attempted to look believable until the twitch of her lips betrayed her. She giggled and watched a slow smile bloom across his lips.

Voices echoed up the stairway, and the intimate moment was interrupted. Zach held the door open for her, and they went out into the cold night air.

Another couple was talking quietly next to one of the buggies parked out front. Grace and Zach left them to their private conversation and walked down the drive toward the road.

They'd gone several yards before Grace realized soft snowflakes were falling from the sky. Her breath caught.

The same wonder she felt was reflected on Zach's face.

They left behind the house and buggies and turned down the lane that would take them home. By the time they'd walked a quarter mile, a thin layer of snow covered the ground.

She couldn't resist any longer and spun in a circle beneath the snow, her arms thrown wide. She sensed Zach watching her before she stopped, wrapping her arms around herself and beaming at him.

"I'm such a ninny." She spoke the words a little breathlessly.

"No, you're not." But he didn't move any closer to her. "You find simple joys around you. It's something I like about you."

Warmth bloomed inside her, making up for each tiny bite of icy cold against her skin. He looked chagrined, like maybe he hadn't meant to say that aloud. Whether he had meant it or not, she wasn't going to let him take it back.

"What's not to be joyful about?" Her heart twinged at the thought of Sarah's grief, but she quickly squelched that thought. "I've just spent time with *goot* friends. And now I'm dancing in the snow with a man I admire."

Something sparked in his eyes. Maybe vulnerability. Maybe hope.

When his voice emerged, it was hoarse and low. "You are?"

She held out both hands. He hesitated only briefly and then stepped forward, clasping her hands in his. "Like this?"

She gave a gentle tug until they were both spinning slowly under the falling snow, their hands acting as an axis like the center of a wooden top. She knew there was a beautiful landscape around them. The snow blanketed quiet fields and turned the treetops into works of art. But all she could see was the man before her. The smile that bloomed and grew across his face. The warmth in his eyes, directed at her.

She laughed in sheer abandon.

Whatever this was growing between them, Zach felt it, too. She was sure of it.

Slowly, their spinning stopped. And slowly they drew closer to each other. He was still holding her hands, and he gently drew her near. Near enough that his shoulders blocked the breeze. She had to tilt her head up to look at him.

Snowflakes stuck in his eyelashes, clumping them together. The look he gave her was both tender and uncertain. He leaned closer.

"Grace, I don't know—" He breathed the words.

"Oh, Gracie!"

Zach broke away quickly at the sound of Violet's voice calling out. Grace and Zach must've paused long enough for her sisters to catch up to them. They were hurrying along under the curtain of snow that was falling more rapidly now.

"What are you two up to?" Violet's words were teasing, and though her arm was locked with Sarah's, it didn't stop her from joining Zach and Grace.

Sarah's eyes were dark, her expression unreadable. Grace sent her sister an apologetic look, but Sarah's gaze skipped completely over her.

Zach had gone tense beside her. A glance at his face showed he'd erased all emotion from his expression, his eyes shuttered and closed off.

Grace knew the interruption must've been intentional. Sarah must've seen them leaving the Troyers' house together.

Grace's disappointment at the interruption of her tender moment with Zach was tempered with guilt. She should've spoken to Sarah before now. She didn't want to hurt her sister.

But she also didn't want to hurt Zach. She took his arm, leaning close to him, both for warm and to offer connection. She didn't want this to be the end of their time together. When they arrived home, maybe she could convince him to come inside for some hot chocolate.

But she didn't have the chance. At the porch steps, he said a polite goodbye to both her and her sisters and left.

Grace watched him cross the yard to the *daadi haus* and couldn't help but wonder what would've happened if her sisters hadn't interrupted them. Would he have kissed her? She'd wanted his kiss. It would be her first. And she wanted it to be Zach.

# Chapter Fourteen

The house was quiet as Grace readied for bed. She'd expected to be confronted by Sarah immediately, but that hadn't happened.

*Mamm* and *Daed* had been in bed when they'd returned from the singing and so had the boys. But now she'd let down her hair and brushed it out, washed her face and donned her nightdress, and Sarah still hadn't come upstairs.

Was she avoiding Grace? The distance between them that had grown over the past few weeks made Grace ache for the closeness they'd once had.

If Sarah wouldn't come to her, she would go to Sarah.

She found Sarah in the kitchen downstairs, standing at the counter. She was drinking a glass of water. She had to have noticed Grace's approach.

Grace cleared her throat.

But Sarah continued to stare out the darkened window.

"Are you okay?" Grace asked quietly. She was aware of her family sleeping upstairs.

Sarah still didn't look at her. "I never thought you would betray me."

Grace flinched. How was caring about someone a betrayal?

She thought about Zach's touch. The clasp of his hands on hers. The vulnerability in his gaze when he'd drawn close to her.

Sarah would never experience any of that with Thomas again. Grace ached for her sister.

"I didn't expect for this to happen," she said. She'd seen a lonely young man and wanted to offer friendship, but somewhere in the course of time they'd spent together, her feelings for Zach had deepened.

Sarah began to turn away.

"Please, would you listen to me?" Grace demanded.

Sarah spun to face her, eyes flashing. "You need to listen. Everyone at the Troyers' was talking about you tonight."

Sarah's glass landed on the counter with a clunk. "They were all whispering about you. You turned down Reuben and Jonah to walk home with the man who killed Thomas. What did you expect?"

Grace's hands were shaking, and she closed them into fists at her sides. "That's not fair. Zach paid for his mistakes."

He wasn't a hardened criminal who'd made repeated offenses. He'd made bad choices as a teen, but he wasn't making them anymore.

He was the man who was patient with Isaiah, playing countless games of checkers just to make a little boy happy. He was the man who found joy in simple things, like holding a puppy. He'd survived a difficult childhood, and she saw the way he still questioned his worth.

"Not fair?" Sarah's voice shook, her emotions finally breaking through. "Not fair? I lost the only man I will ever love. I lost my chance for a family. I'll never hold a baby of my own. I'll never teach my little girl to bake cookies. I'll never fall asleep beside Thomas. Zach took that from me."

Grace shuddered at the despair and rage in Sarah's voice. Her heart went out to her sister. She'd known Sarah's grief ran deep. She didn't know what to say, how to offer comfort to her sister's despair. Sarah believed her life was over, but Grace knew that God could work miracles. Maybe there was even still someone out there for Sarah. But right now her sister was locked in so much pain and anger...

Grace hesitated for too long.

Sarah lashed out again. "How can you choose *him* over your own sister?"

Grace recoiled from the heat of Sarah's temper. They'd fought as children, but never like this. "I'm not choosing him. Why does it have to be a choice? Of course I choose you. You're my sister."

But Sarah shook her head.

"If you would just give him a chance," Grace went on. "You would see he's—"

"Give him a chance?" Sarah hissed. "I told you I'd seen him with his *Englisher* friends. But you didn't listen. He's not who you think he is." Sarah paced away from the counter and then back. "What do I have to do—?"

It happened almost in slow motion. Sarah thrust out one hand and knocked over the African violet on the windowsill. It bounced off the corner of the counter and then fell to the floor. The pot shattered, scattering dirt across the floor. The plant lay in broken pieces, leaves sheared away from the force.

Her plant! It had been one of the first plants Grace had propagated herself. A gift for *Mamm* on a long-ago birthday. Sarah was so angry. Was it an accident that she'd knocked it to the floor?

Grace stood and stared at the mess, stunned. Sarah was frozen in place, too. From far away, she thought she heard a floorboard creak. And then the soft snick of the back door closing. Maybe she imagined it. Everything was still and quiet, only the sound of Sarah's ragged breathing and the thud of her own heartbeat in her ears.

Grace knelt on the cold floor, her hands going to the broken leaves.

Her pulse pounded in her ears. She expected a quick apology from her sister. But Sarah stood over her, silent and still.

They had never had a gulf between them this wide. She didn't know whether she could bridge it. Or if her relationship with Sarah could be repaired.

Sarah took one more ragged breath. She still didn't offer to help, holding herself carefully apart. "You'll see. Time will tell, and *everyone* will see what kind of person Zach is."

Shaken and uncertain, Grace kept her head down as Sarah padded out of the room.

She carefully picked up the broken leaves. One clump of the original plant remained. It would need babying, but it would survive. One day, it would be full and bloom again.

Zach was like one of her broken plants, she thought. Life had tried to break him, but he'd returned to the Amish faith. He was part of a community that would offer him the support he needed to flourish again.

Would her relationship with Sarah be the same? Right now it felt broken, jagged edges that could so easily cut them apart. But with the right care and nourishment, could the relationship grow whole again?

She would clean up this mess, sweep the floor and pick up the pieces of the shattered pot. It would take some time to repot the plant and nurture the broken leaves. For now, she clipped the ragged edges of each stem and rested them in a bowl of water. She found a chipped bowl in the back of one upper cabinet and silently apologized to *Mamm* as she scooped what dirt she could gather from the floor and tucked the broken plant and what was left of its root ball in the bowl. Tomorrow when she could go inside the *daadi haus* without disturbing Zach, she would plant the leaves in their own pots and repot the plant.

Her familiar actions didn't soothe her.

How could she be with Zach when it hurt Sarah so deeply?

*Everyone will see what kind of person Zach is.* Sarah's words sent a shiver through her.

How could she walk away from Zach when

she'd seen the spark of light in his eyes just this afternoon?

Just thinking about it made her ache. Her heart wanted Zach.

But Sarah had to come first.

Days after the singing, Zach riffled through the shop's first aid kit, a small plastic tub that Mr. Beiler kept on a high shelf in the small kitchen area. It was the end of the workday, and he had nicked himself with an awl, resulting in a cut in the fleshy part between thumb and forefinger on his left hand. He didn't need stitches, but he didn't want his blood to stain any of Mr. Beiler's projects.

His distraction had caused the injury, and he was angry with himself. Deeper than that, he was angry with himself because he had let himself believe that he might have a real chance to win Grace's heart.

The sound of the pneumatic saw faded, and Zach knew the other men would be wrapping up their final jobs to go home for the day. Zach would've stayed all night if he could.

"You all right?" Amos stepped into the room, letting the door swing half closed behind him.

Zach nodded, his jaw locked tight. As long as he didn't say the words, it wasn't a lie.

He wasn't all right. He hadn't been all right

since he'd overheard the argument between Sarah and Grace on the night of the singing.

He wasn't supposed to have heard it. When he'd walked Grace to her door, they hadn't had a chance to say more than a cursory goodbye, but somehow when he had been taking off his coat in the *daadi haus*, he'd found one of Grace's mittens in his pocket. He didn't remember taking it from her, but they had clasped hands on the porch. Regardless of how it had ended up on his person, he wanted to return it to her in case she needed it tomorrow.

He'd only stepped into the mudroom to place it on top of the shelf of cubbies, but then he'd heard voices and frozen, afraid of being discovered. Once he'd realized they were talking about him, he'd been even more afraid to move. He didn't want to give Sarah another reason to be angry at Grace, didn't want to see the dawning realization in Grace's expression. Because Sarah was right.

*Zach took that from me.* He'd heard the pain in Sarah's voice as she'd described the future he'd ripped away from her.

He'd slipped outside before Grace had answered, but he knew there was no way she would choose him over her sister. Zach wasn't worth a broken relationship between the sisters.

He was standing on the Beilers' back porch,

breathless with hurt, when he heard something shatter. He'd been startled. But the house had remained dark and still.

"You've been quiet all week," Amos said now. "Quieter than usual, anyway."

His friend cracked a smile, but Zach ducked his head, pretending to focus on applying the sticky bandage over his wound.

He missed Grace.

He'd hadn't seen her all week. He'd bought a dozen eggs and a loaf of bread at the grocery shop in town and taken his breakfast alone in the *daadi haus*. He'd taken on a job putting new brakes on a car for an *Englisher* family in town. The job had allowed him an excuse to be away from the Beilers' home during suppertime for two nights in a row.

The worst part was that Grace was avoiding him, too.

He'd asked Mr. Beiler whether he could come in late yesterday morning. He'd planned to ride his bike to work. Grace had been approaching the *daadi haus* as he'd left. She must've wanted the time to work with her violets.

She'd stopped dead in the middle of the yard, a panicked look on her face.

He'd swallowed back whatever greeting he might've called out and got on his bike as quickly as he could. He didn't look back as he pedaled away.

Before her fight with Sarah, she'd called him a friend. Zach had wanted more. Had held on to a desperate hope that he wasn't bound by his past.

He was a fool.

When he'd been a naive teenager, he had let selfishness rule him. And look what damage he'd done.

He cared about Grace. He couldn't help it.

And she deserved so much more than the pain his friendship would cause her. He didn't know whether he could forgive himself if he cost her the relationship with Sarah.

"Zach. Are you still in there?"

He'd been so lost in his thoughts that he hadn't realized Amos had moved across the room and was close enough to give him a friendly pat on the shoulder. For a moment, Zach's brain got lost in the jagged maze of his memories from the last four years, and he flinched as if Amos had been one of the prison guards and his friendly touch had been a rough push.

"It's just me." Amos held his hands up in front of him. He backed up.

"Sorry," Zach mumbled. "I guess I am distracted today."

"It's not just today." Amos's face was creased in concern. "What's going on? I want to help."

Of course, Amos knew that Zach had walked Grace home. But Zach had kept everything else to himself. And he wasn't going to confide in Amos now. Amos was Grace's cousin. He was family. Even if he would understand Grace's dilemma, Zach couldn't share what was private between the two sisters.

"I...don't think it's going to work out between Grace and me."

"What?" Amos was genuinely shocked. "I know she likes you."

Days ago, his words might've made Zach's heart leap with hope. But today there was only an ugly fullness blocking his chest.

"There are other things she has to consider."

Amos's brow furrowed. Silence fell between them. They stood side by side, leaning against the tall counter. Zach stared ahead, not really seeing the room in front of him. He waited for Amos to say what he'd been thinking for the past few days.

For once, Amos remained silent.

So Zach said it. "Maybe I should leave Walnut Cove."

Amos was shocked all over again. He shook his head. "Maybe you should talk to Grace."

And give her a chance to say she never wanted to see him again?

"If you won't talk to her," Amos said, "at least talk to her *daed*."

He'd barely begun to mull over the idea when a blond head in a prayer *kapp* peeked around the door.

Grace.

His heart stumbled in his chest, and he couldn't stop the rush of affection quickly followed by a hot knot blocking his throat.

She gave a tight smile and stepped into the room. Her eyes dropped before she glanced in Zach's direction.

"This came in the mail for you," she said softly. It took a moment to register she was talking to him, because she still wasn't looking at him. "I know how important finding your *onkle* has been."

She crossed the room, keeping distance between them like he had in the very beginning. And it hurt.

He tried not to feel anything as she extended a postcard to him. He took it from her, his gaze falling to the scrolled handwriting on the plain white card.

*Your uncle lives in Columbus now.*

Scrolled beneath was an address. Columbus. A two-hour bus ride.

The signature on the bottom was one Zach didn't recognize, not until he remembered visiting Paul's rental house. The woman who lived there now had promised to check with the landlord. Zach had left the Beilers' address with her since he didn't have a phone.

Amos, nosy busybody that he was, had leaned over Zach's shoulder to read the postcard.

"Are you going to see him?"

Zach didn't know. Tomorrow was Saturday, and he would have the time free from work. Maybe it was a sign that the postcard had come today, when he had been considering leaving Walnut Cove.

"You might need a friend," Amos suggested quietly.

Grace watched him with compassion. When Zach met her gaze, she quickly dropped her eyes.

Amos missed none of it. He jerked his chin toward Grace. "You might even need two. Grace, you should come with us. Can your *mamm* spare you tomorrow?"

He wanted to bark at Amos, but Grace's soft gaze stopped him. He hadn't even decided whether he was going. Having Grace along would be more painful than helpful.

But when she murmured a soft assent, he couldn't take back Amos's invitation. Even though he wanted to.

# Chapter Fifteen

Grace stood on the sidewalk between Zach and Amos. The three of them stared at the small, dingy house. None of the houses on this street were particularly well maintained, but this one was somehow more shabby than the rest. The yard was overgrown. One of the windowpanes had been broken, and now a piece of cardboard was taped over it. It was midmorning, but the windows were dark. It made the whole place seem gloomy.

Zach stood looking at the house, making no move to cross the yard and knock.

She glanced at his face, but whatever he was feeling was kept inside. His expression was shuttered and empty.

On the bus ride here, he had been quiet and pensive. He had spent much of the two hours staring out the window at the passing scenery.

Amos and Grace had kept up a running conversation, occasionally drawing him in. Each time, she'd noted the darkness in his eyes before he'd turned his face back to the window. How could she explain? Sarah needed her. It didn't matter what Grace wanted.

Sarah was finally speaking to her again, though she had spent the past few days working feverishly at her chores. She'd been secretive about a trip to town, but Grace had been too down to ask *Mamm* if she knew what Sarah was up to.

She shouldn't have come today. But she'd remembered the way Zach had spoken of his *onkle*. This couldn't be easy for him. Surely Sarah couldn't fault her for being a good friend. Not that she'd told Sarah where she was going today. *Mamm* and Sarah had gone to visit *Aendi* Martha, and Grace hoped to return before they got home.

Now Zach shivered, and she didn't think it was from the biting wind. She'd brought along sandwiches and a thermos of *kaffee*. Those were long gone. But right now, Grace wished there was some *kaffee* left. Zach looked as if he needed something to brace him.

Amos, perceptive as usual, said, "You don't have to go in. We can just go back to the bus station."

Grace had been thinking the same thing. Zach looked haunted. The same way he'd looked when he had showed up on their doorstep. She hadn't realized how much of his tension had disappeared over the past few weeks. The time in Walnut Cove had made his smile come more easily.

Now it looked like he was grinding his teeth. "Yes, I do," he finally said.

Why? From what little he had told her about his *onkle*, the man didn't seem like the type who would be waiting with welcome arms. He hadn't even come to see Zach in prison. Hadn't cared enough to let Zach know when he moved. She couldn't understand this need to see his *onkle*, but she had come this far and she was going to stand by his side. Family was complicated. How well she knew that.

In the front window, the one with the broken pane in one corner, a head and shoulders appeared, looking out toward them.

It was not a man-size head and shoulders. Unless Grace was mistaken, it was a little girl.

Amos seemed oblivious, but Zach went completely still.

Her toes were going numb. She didn't know who the little girl was or who she might be to Zach's *onkle*, but if he was insistent on going inside, then they should go.

Zach strode forward to cross the lawn.

She and Amos followed, standing a step be-hind and beside him as he knocked on the door.

She could hear the patter of little footsteps and a high-pitched voice call out, though she couldn't make out the words. Zach was barely breathing.

There was a prolonged moment before they heard heavier footsteps.

And then the door opened to reveal an older man in a stained T-shirt and jeans that had seen better days. Salt-and-pepper stubble covered his cheeks and jaw.

He squinted at Zach, his eyes cold. "You got out, huh?"

She didn't know what she had expected. Maybe a smile. Maybe a kind word. Which seemed foolish in the face of what little Zach had revealed about this man.

Zach didn't say anything. She was slightly behind him and he was taller than her, and she couldn't get a glimpse of his expression. All she could see was his *onkle*'s frown. All she could feel was an echo of their past.

"What do you want? A handout?"

Zach inhaled softly, like the words had been a physical blow. He still didn't speak.

It was Amos who spoke. "It was a two-hour

trip down here. Do you mind if we come in for a little bit before we head back to the bus station?"

Paul's gaze finally flicked to Amos and Grace, registering their presence behind Zach. He took in everything. Her dress, her prayer *kapp*, Amos's suspenders.

Finally, he swung the door wider and stepped back.

For a second, she wasn't sure Zach was going to go inside. But he stepped over the threshold.

The cold drove her in close behind him. She bumped him, and when he turned to check on her, she saw that though his face was expressionless, everything was visible in his eyes. They burned. Whether from grief or hurt, she didn't know.

She couldn't think about Sarah. There was only Zach, hurting and holding himself apart.

That wouldn't do.

She slid her hand into his cold one and clasped it tight.

Zach didn't know what he was doing. Part of him was still outside on the sidewalk, asking, *why did I come here?*

Amos was right. He didn't *have* to see Paul. But he had questions. And inside him was still a terrified seventeen-year-old, wondering why his uncle had left him to the system.

He didn't know whether there was any chance for reconciliation between himself and Paul. But he had to try, didn't he?

And then he'd seen a small face in the window. Who was she?

He felt shaken. That was the only excuse for keeping Grace's hand as he followed his uncle into the tiny, shabby living room. There was the same old battered couch where he'd done homework as a boy. Who would waste the effort to move such an ugly old thing? Half its springs had been missing from beneath the cushions back when Zach had last sat on it.

Somehow he ended up squished in the middle of Amos and Grace sitting on the couch. None of them had taken off their coats. Zach felt as if he might start to suffocate in his, but he didn't let go of Grace to shrug it off.

His uncle sat in a sad recliner that had seen better days. His eyes were narrowed and focused on Zach.

Zach had to swallow twice before he could get words out. "I'm sorry for all the mistakes I made. For the drinking and the partying."

It was what he had come here to say.

His uncle looked surprised. And then his eyes narrowed farther. "Did you get religion or something behind bars?"

In the face of Zach's apology, the words were

a verbal slap. He didn't feel them, not really. Once he had stepped foot in the house, a sort of numbness had stolen over him.

Over the past two days, he'd thought that maybe he should leave Walnut Cove. And then yesterday, looking at that postcard, he'd had a wild thought that maybe he could stay with Paul for a few weeks to get on his feet. That's what he'd planned to ask—beg—for when he'd been released from prison.

But he couldn't come back here. Even if his uncle would offer, unlikely as that seemed, Zach didn't belong here anymore. Maybe he never had.

"I came back to the faith my *mamm* and *daed* taught me." He said the words calmly, but something flashed in Paul's eyes. It was gone so quickly that Zach couldn't be sure what emotion it was.

Maybe he would never see his uncle again after today. He'd come seeking closure. And answers.

"Why didn't you come see me? Or write to me?" he asked.

Paul coughed, the sound dry and hacking. "You weren't my problem no more."

That stung. Zach had always known his uncle found him a burden to be borne, but for Paul to say it so blatantly…well, it hurt.

"If you need money, you should look somewhere else." Paul coughed again, muffling the sound by keeping his mouth closed.

He didn't. Because of Mr. Beiler's generosity, Zach had been able to save a small nest egg.

Was that the only reason his uncle could think of that Zach would want to see him?

There was nothing here for him, Zach realized. He might share a blood connection with his uncle, but that didn't make them a family. He had thought he'd begun to discover true family in Walnut Cove. Amos. Isaiah. Mr. Beiler.

Grace.

In the span of a few short weeks, they had been more family to him than his uncle ever had. But that was gone, too. He couldn't think about that now.

He was getting ready to find his feet and walk out of there when a small girl entered the room, padding in with bare feet. She scurried across the room to stand hidden behind Paul's recliner, peeking out at the three visitors.

Getting a closer look at her, Zach's stomach took a free fall. Her hair was the same chestnut brown that he had seen in the mirror as a child. It fell between her chin and shoulder, and he could see that it hadn't been brushed today—maybe in a couple of days—because there was a tangle visible from here. She had a smudge on one cheek, and it bothered him that her feet were bare. He could feel how drafty this room was, even wearing a coat.

But it was her eyes that snagged his focus. He'd seen those eyes not long ago. She had Tiffany's eyes.

He couldn't stop looking at her. Thoughts tumbled in his head, coming fast and out of order, like his brain was caught in a tornado. How old was she? She had to be a little older than three, didn't she? She couldn't be Tiffany's daughter. Could she?

"Hello," Grace said softly. "Who are you?"

Realization was swamping him. He tried to let go of Grace's hand, but she glanced at him and then held fast.

At Grace's question, the girl shrank back even more behind the chair.

Paul's expression was cool. "This? This is Kinley. Zach's daughter."

His words were confirmation of every thought bombarding Zach.

It couldn't be.

He'd seen Tiffany two weeks ago. A lifetime ago, as time stretched and warped in his head.

He had a daughter? And his daughter lived with the man who had considered Zach a problem. A burden.

Zach could feel blood pumping beneath the

skin of his face, skin that felt stretched too tight. He was aware of Grace and Amos beside him, witnessing this horrific moment. Now they would know another of his sins. Here was even more reason for Grace to stay away from him.

"Why—how is she here with you?" Zach heard his own voice as if from far away.

Paul started to speak, then apparently thought better of it. He turned to the girl. "Why don't you go get some cereal or something?"

Connected to Grace as he was, Zach felt the slight movement from her. Like she wanted to follow Kinley as she crept into the kitchen, giving them one last look over her shoulder. Did Grace think the little one was too young to be taking care of herself?

She was too young, but Zach couldn't even wrap his head around it.

At least his uncle had thought to spare her feelings for whatever he was getting ready to say. "That girlfriend of yours, Tiffany, showed up a few months after your conviction. Told me she was pregnant and that it was yours. She couldn't keep it."

*It.* That was how Paul referred to Zach's daughter?

His uncle shrugged. "I told her I was done raising kids, but she begged and begged."

And at some point, Paul had given in.

No. It couldn't be real. Tiffany had been self-centered. Zach could recognize that now, after he had been forced to face so much of the ugliness inside himself. But he'd shared secrets with her. How many times had he told her about Paul's neglect? At least a dozen. She wouldn't have just given up her child—their child—into his care. Would she?

Maybe Zach should be glad that his daughter hadn't gone into the foster system. Right now he didn't know what to feel. His insides were full of confusing emotions. This news was too big to digest.

He realized he was squeezing Grace's hand too hard. He couldn't think about depending on her. She wasn't for him.

He let go.

"Does she know about me?" His voice sounded rough even to his own ears.

"Why should she? You aren't a part of her life." Paul stood up. "I think we're done here. I told you I'm not giving you any money, and there's nothing left to say."

*No. Please—* "Can I talk to her? To Kinley?" Her name on his lips was strange and new and somehow painful. He needed to know if she was all right.

"Nah. It's time for you to leave."

He wanted to protest. He wanted to shout.

But Amos gave him a tight-lipped shake of his head. Grace stood up. He followed suit.

Zach left the house and followed his friends down the sidewalk. The numbness he'd felt a short time ago was gone, replaced with fear and anger and a whole host of emotions he didn't know how to express.

He sent one last glance over his shoulder at the terrible house with its dark windows. This time he knew that his daughter was inside.

Was he really supposed to just walk away?

But he didn't have a choice.

# *Chapter Sixteen*

"Where do you think you're going?"

*Mamm*'s stern question startled Grace and stopped her short as she was donning her coat and mittens in the mudroom. It was early Monday morning. The sun wouldn't be up for another half hour. But Grace had spent a sleepless night worrying about Zach. She'd come downstairs in the early morning hours to keep from waking Sarah and had seen a bobbing light out the kitchen window, glowing around the side of the barn. It had to be Zach, and she needed to talk to him.

And that's when *Mamm* startled her.

"I need to speak with Zach," she told *Mamm* now, buttoning her coat.

"It's too early. It's inappropriate for you to go over to the *daadi haus* now." *Mamm* stood in the doorway with a shawl wrapped around her shoulders. Her hair had been tucked hastily into her prayer *kapp*.

"I saw his light down by the barn. He must be working on the greenhouse." She'd walked down to the barn late last week, and the plastic had been stretched over the frame and the door installed.

*Mamm* reached out one hand as if to stop Grace. Her brow creased in concern. "Are you certain it's him out there? I'd better go get your *daed*."

"Who else would it be?" Grace didn't share her mother's concern.

But *Mamm* bit her lip and hesitated before saying, "Someone was causing trouble at the shop again. There were marks on the door like someone had tried to break in. And more beer cans."

What? Shock coursed through Grace. She shivered at the thought of someone trying to break into *Daed*'s shop. Why would someone do that?

"I know it's Zach out there. He's been working on the greenhouse, though I don't know why he's working so early today." She could guess. He hadn't attended worship services yesterday. She hadn't seen him at all after the near-silent bus ride home from Columbus. She was worried about him.

*Mamm* frowned. "I don't like how you and Sarah have been fighting these past weeks."

Grace's heart lurched. She'd sneaked out of the room this morning. And last night, she'd avoided being alone with Sarah so she wouldn't have to evade any questions about her whereabouts on Saturday.

"If she wakes up, don't tell her I'm out there."

*Mamm*'s frown grew. "Young lady—"

"I just need a few minutes with him."

*Mamm* sighed. "You can go, but I'm sending your *daed* out in a few minutes."

It certainly wasn't acceptance, but Grace didn't argue further. She slipped out into the dark, flashlight in hand.

*Mamm*'s worry that it might be someone other than Zach sneaking around made Grace cautious, and she peeked around the corner of the barn before she rounded it. The lamplight shone from inside the greenhouse, and she heard movement from behind the opaque plastic sheeting. It was Zach after all.

Yesterday had been a blur of worship and dinner and then family time at home. Zach had been absent from all of it. Her heart hurt, thinking about his loneliness.

He looked up when she pushed through the door. The wind was biting, so she closed the door behind her. Without any source of heat, the greenhouse was still cold, but at least it protected them from the wind.

Zach had strung a battery-powered lamp overhead. In its light, she could see his eyes were shuttered before he went back to his work.

"Hallo, Zach. I missed you yesterday." It was the truth, but she hadn't meant to say it.

He flinched, even as he kept his eyes on the peg he was inserting to connect one of the shelves to its brace. "I needed some time to think."

Of course he had. He'd been hit with a big revelation. He had a daughter. She was still trying to wrap her mind around it.

When the silence stretched between them, she asked, "How can I help?"

"I've got this. I'll cut more shelves after work. I should finish up tomorrow."

She could see that. Zach had been busy out here. Shelves lined the far wall, and he was halfway through the longer wall that ran parallel to the barn.

"That's not what I meant."

His hands were shaking as he picked up another peg and then reached for a board from the stack on the floor. "I can handle things on my own."

"Why should you, when you've got—" *me?*
"—a community around you?" She wanted to

be the one to help him, but thoughts of Sarah made her hesitate.

A muscle ticked in his cheek.

She wanted to reach out and hold his hand, the way she had in his *onkle*'s house. But she didn't.

She glanced to the side, back toward the house if she had been outside the greenhouse.

Zach noticed, and the muscles around his mouth tightened. "You should go. Before anyone sees you out here."

What did that mean?

"*Mamm* knows I'm out here."

He manipulated a peg, leaning in and twisting it when it didn't want to set correctly. "I've got a lot to deal with. You didn't know about Kinley when we—when you walked with me. It didn't mean anything. It was just one walk."

His words made her breath catch with hurt.

It had meant something to her. She wanted to argue with him. Force him to admit that he wasn't being truthful. But Sarah's voice in her head stopped her.

How could she build up his hopes when she couldn't see a way forward? Not unless Sarah relented and forgave him.

So she said nothing.

But she picked up the next peg that he would need and held it out to him. He looked at her for a long moment before he accepted it, tension coiling around them, almost palpable.

"What are you going to do about Kinley?"

"I don't know." He didn't look at her as he adjusted the next shelf. "I don't know if I should do anything."

"You should talk to *Daed*."

As if she'd called him with her quiet words, she heard the crunch of footsteps on the grass outside. The sun was coming up, lighting the horizon with gold.

"Grace? Zach?"

She moved to the door and opened it for *Daed*. "We're here."

*Daed* looked past Grace, examining the interior without entering. "It looks *goot* out here. But maybe too small for three people at once."

Grace glanced at Zach, who still avoided her gaze. Gone was the easy camaraderie they'd shared at the Sunday singing. Her stomach knotted.

"Maybe we can catch up later," she said to Zach.

He only shook his head.

She left feeling desperate. Zach obviously needed a friend. It didn't bother her that he had a daughter. Not really. He'd been very clear that he'd repented of the way he'd acted four years ago.

Did he still have feelings for Kinley's mother? Zach had told her that his friends had abandoned him after his incarceration. But he'd never mentioned her specifically. It had been obvious during the few minutes inside Paul's house that Zach hadn't known about his daughter. Paul had said he'd never told Kinley about Zach.

But just because the woman had been absent from Zach's life didn't mean he didn't still think about her.

She wished she could ask him about it. But she'd been the one to step back, afraid of hurting Sarah worse.

Why would Zach share anything with her now?

Zach wanted to call out after Grace. He'd seen the way she'd blanched when he'd said their time together hadn't meant anything. The last thing he wanted to do was hurt her, but it ripped his insides to shreds just being near her.

She wasn't for him. The sooner they both got it through their heads, the better. He hadn't known it before, but he was a dad. That was another strike against him. Another reason for a good woman like Grace to stay far away from him.

Was her father here to ask Zach to leave?

"You weren't at worship yesterday," Mr. Beiler said. "I was worried about you."

He was? That hurt, too. Mr. Beiler cared about him. He must, in some way. There was no caginess in the man's expression. Only genuine concern. It made Zach's chest tight and hot.

And all of a sudden, his confusing emotions overflowed.

"I had some news when I visited my uncle on Saturday. I wasn't sure what to do about it. I'm still not."

As usual, Mr. Beiler did not rush to fill the silence. He left Zach to flounder and then eventually blurt it out.

"I have a daughter. Kinley."

Mr. Beiler's brows raised in clear surprise. "Why didn't you tell me this before?"

Zach shook his head, still feeling an echo of the shock he'd felt at seeing the young girl on Saturday. "I didn't know about her. Her mother was my girlfriend before—before the accident. She didn't tell me." He didn't understand why Tiffany had kept silent about Kinley. All it would've taken was a phone call to let him know in prison. Or she could've told him weeks ago when she'd showed up at the Beilers' house.

"I haven't been with anyone else," he said. "If you want me to leave right away, I'll understand."

The thought of never seeing Grace again opened a hollow ache inside him.

"Why would I want that? Are you the same man you once were?"

Zach shook his head. He had wanted to lock his past away, move beyond it. But it seemed his past wouldn't go away.

Mr. Beiler waited for him to speak again.

Zach put his hands in his pockets to warm them. It was too awkward to maneuver the pegs into place with gloves on, but now that he wasn't actively working, his hands were stiffening in the cold.

"I don't know what to do," he admitted. "About Kinley. My uncle wouldn't even let me talk to her."

Mr. Beiler let a moment lapse. "What do you want to do?"

"I don't even know if Paul is taking good care of her." He could still remember that tangle in her hair. Kinley's bare feet when it had been drafty and cold in the dilapidated house. Paul telling the three-year-old to make her own cereal.

He never should've walked away.

But he was a stranger to her. She'd been shy and fearful. She didn't know him. That was his fault. If he'd been in Walnut Cove instead of in prison, Tiffany would've come to him. He would've been a part of Kinley's life from the beginning.

His stomach cramped, thinking of the things he'd missed. Her birth. Holding her as an infant. Her first steps. Her first smile.

She hadn't smiled once yesterday.

"I can't just leave her there with him." He said the words aloud, and the realization settled inside him, firm and right. "He wasn't kind to me." It was the first time he'd said as much to Mr. Beiler, and the words almost caught in his throat. He had to clear it to be able to speak again. "I don't want that for her."

Mr. Beiler considered his words. "You will have to work twice as hard as anyone else. But it will be worth it. Each of my children has been a blessing from *Gott*."

An instantaneous thought of Grace holding a baby in her arms rose in his mind's eye. She would be a loving mother. He quashed the thought ruthlessly.

"What do I do now?" he asked.

"Have you prayed about it?"

He had. But his prayers didn't seem to reach any higher than the ceiling.

Mr. Beiler moved closer to the shelves Zach was constructing. They were designed so each shelf supported the one above it. More shelves could be added, making the structure taller, or removed as needed. Amos had helped Zach sketch out the design and figure out what the measurements should be.

His face got hot as Mr. Beiler reached out to touch the top shelf that Zach had just installed. Mr. Beiler wiggled it, and thankfully, it held. Mr. Beiler touched the hole where the next peg would connect another shelf. What did he think of Zach's work? He was a master craftsman. He'd once told Zach that he'd learned from his father, who had moved to Walnut Cove when Mr. Beiler had been a teen and started the business here.

Zach wished for the kind of legacy behind Mr. Beiler's business.

Finally, Mr. Beiler turned back to Zach. "This is *goot* work. It is *goot* because you made *goot* plans. You did not rush as you collected and shaped each piece."

What was he saying? That Zach shouldn't rush into things with Kinley? He hated the thought of her being under Paul's care. What if she was hungry, right this very moment? What if Paul didn't care?

"You can come in late today," Mr. Beiler said. "Why don't you ride over to the Bontragers' and use their barn phone to call your *onkle*? You can start planning when you know where things stand."

Zach's stomach performed a slow flip at the thought. It wouldn't take long to bike over to the neighbors'.

He could bring Kinley home to Walnut Cove. The thought filled him with joy and terror. Here was his chance to have a legacy. To have the family he longed for.

But there was a part of him still filled with a hollow ache. Lately, when he'd thought about family, he'd thought about Grace.

He already knew she wasn't for him. This was just further proof. How could he expect her to want another woman's child?

# *Chapter Seventeen*

Zach was shaking as he kicked his leg over the bicycle seat and pushed it the last few feet up to the Bontragers' plank fence. He leaned the bike carefully against the fence and slipped into the Bontragers' barn, where the family kept a phone. They had given permission to the Beilers and other close neighbors to use it if needed. Zach had met the family at Sunday worship, and since this morning's phone call had been Mr. Beiler's idea, he didn't go up to the house and knock.

The barn was empty except for two milk cows. In the quiet, Zach could hear his heart thudding in his ears.

He picked up the receiver and looked at the number that Amos had cajoled Uncle Paul into giving up in case of emergency, just before they'd left the house on Saturday. Amos had scribbled it on a scrap of paper, and now Zach's fingers trembled as he read it off and dialed.

He felt out of sorts, as if the world was tipping on its axis. Everything was going to change.

What would Kinley think of him? She didn't know him. It was possible that Paul had filled her head with lies about Zach. He didn't try to tell himself that this would be easy.

But in his heart, he knew it was right. Kinley needed him.

He pressed the receiver to his ear and listened to the faint ring on the other end.

It rang twice before his uncle answered. "Hello?"

There was a tinny sound of voices in the background, as if Paul's TV was on. Zach had to swallow hard before he could speak. "Paul? It's Zach."

There was a beat of silence. "Didn't think I'd be hearing from you again."

He'd thought wrong. Had Paul imagined Zach would just abandon his daughter?

"I'm calling about Kinley. I want to— When can I come and get her?"

The blaring sound of the TV on his uncle's end died out. "What are you talking about?"

Zach closed his eyes. Of course Paul wasn't going to make this easy.

"I want Kinley to come live with me."

"What, in a halfway house?"

The anticipation bubbling inside Zach churned, threatening to turn into anger. He tried to breathe, reminded himself that getting angry at Paul's rudeness wouldn't solve anything. "I've been renting a place in Walnut Cove." It was easier than explaining about the Beilers' kindness. "There's plenty of room for the both of us."

"Who's going to watch her while you're at work?"

Zach was stunned that his uncle was arguing with him. *All you do is eat.* Zach remembered vividly the statement and others like it that Paul had thrown at him when he'd been hungry and asked for an after-school snack. Paul had complained about the extra laundry, about buying clothes for a growing boy, about Zach talking too much or getting bad grades. Nothing had ever satisfied his uncle.

Zach had been a burden to him. Why was he putting up a fight about Kinley?

This time it was an effort to keep his voice from shaking. "I haven't worked everything out yet, but I will. She's my daughter. She needs to be with me."

Paul's derisive snort was audible through the phone. He mumbled something that Zach couldn't decipher. Then, "This little girl's mama signed away her rights while you were in prison. I'm not just going to hand her over to you."

Cold dread snaked down Zach's insides and spread with insidious fingers. "That's not right. I never signed anything. I didn't even know about Kinley."

"Don't matter to me. She's my ward now."

Zach didn't understand. He felt flabbergasted at Paul's refusal. All weekend long, as he'd struggled with deciding what to do about the daughter he hadn't known about, he hadn't genuinely considered that Paul might fight him for custody. Given how self-centered his uncle was, Zach had thought he would be happy to be done with the care and expense of a little girl.

"Please." Zach wasn't proud of how his voice shook. "You can't do this."

Paul didn't answer, only hung up the phone.

Zach's eyes blurred with tears, and it took two tries to dial the number again. He got a busy signal, as if his uncle had taken the phone off the hook.

No. It couldn't happen like this.

When he stepped outside, everything seemed all wrong. How could the morning sun be shining like it was? It should be dark and overcast.

He didn't get on his bicycle but pushed it up the driveway and then along the shoulder of the road. He couldn't even think. His mind kept replaying the conversation with Paul. Could he have said anything differently? Should he have apologized again? Or begged?

He was empty and numb when he returned to the Beilers' yard and leaned his bike against the outside of the *daadi haus*. He didn't consciously think it, but his feet took him to the barn, where he found himself standing in front of Bertha and her puppies in their boxed-off stall. His subconscious had brought him to this place where he'd had the most peace since he'd arrived in Walnut Cove.

The puppies were romping and playing, and two of them ran up to greet him, standing on their hind legs with their paws against the hay bale blocking their exit. He scooped up the little girl he'd decided to name Libby. She immediately licked his chin, but he couldn't even find a smile for that.

Several moments later, he heard footsteps.

"Zach?"

Grace. Of course.

He put the puppy down so she could play with her siblings and scrubbed one hand down his face.

Her footsteps got louder as she neared. "I saw you push your bike into the yard and thought you looked upset."

He stared into the stall with his hands at his

sides and tried to breathe. It was easier than looking at her. He didn't want her to witness this.

But his silence didn't deter her. "Zach?"

She touched him. Her fingers slid against the back of his hand, and he shied away. He couldn't bear it.

He swallowed hard, still staring ahead. "Grace, I can't—"

He'd wanted her friendship, and it had been pulled away. He understood why. Of course he did. But it didn't make this hurt any less.

Why was she even here when he'd made it clear that their time together had meant nothing?

*Please, go away.* But of course she didn't hear the unspoken words.

She stayed there, at his side, facing Bertha and the puppies. She spoke softly, "*Daed* said you'd gone over to the Bontragers'. Shall I guess why you needed to use the telephone? I can also guess what your *onkle* had to say."

He squeezed his eyes closed against the onslaught of emotion that wanted to escape. He'd only wanted to remove Kinley from Paul's care. But he'd failed his daughter spectacularly.

Grace had seen Paul in action on Saturday. It wouldn't take much imagination to guess what he'd been like on the phone.

And Zach hated that she knew his shame.

"Please, go away." This time he managed to whisper the words.

Grace's dismay was audible in a tiny inhale. "Zach, I'm sorry."

He could feel the muscle in his jaw ticking. He needed to be alone. He needed to gather himself. He had to get to work. Mr. Beiler was counting on him.

After an interminable few moments, she left. But the absence of her presence didn't help him breathe any easier.

What was he supposed to do now?

He took several more moments trying to compose himself. When he left the barn and went to his bike to ride to Mr. Beiler's shop, a note fluttered in the basket. Grace's handwriting.

*What about Kinley's mother? If you contacted her, maybe she would help.*

Zach had been trying not to think about Tiffany. He was angry that she'd kept this a secret from him. She'd come to find him, and she still hadn't said anything. Why had she kept Kinley a secret?

But suddenly Zach's hope was palpable again. He didn't know where she lived now or her phone number, but Walnut Cove was small enough that someone would know.

And he had Grace to thank for it.

His conflicted heart didn't know what to believe. Grace had sought him out twice today. But that didn't mean she'd chosen him or that she wanted to be with him now that she knew he had a daughter.

Her compassion was too great to let him suffer in silence. That's what it had been in the beginning, and that must be what it was now.

He wanted to feel bitter about it, but he couldn't. His thumb swept across the scrap of paper, across the words she'd penned. If this was all she could give him, it would have to be enough.

## Chapter Eighteen

Grace fought off the tears for as long as she could, but by the time she had carted several loads of violets out to her newly finished greenhouse, she could hold back no longer. She sat on the dirt floor and cried.

She heard the door open and buried her face in her apron, not wanting whoever had come after her to see her tears.

She recognized Sarah's hug as her sister's arm came around her shoulders. Sarah sat on the ground right beside her and hugged her like she had when they had been little kids and Grace had fallen off her bike.

Grace worked to get control of herself until her tears abated to sniffles. When she dabbed at the last of the moisture from her cheeks and raised her head, Sarah was staring at the opaque plastic, her gaze far-off.

"Where did you go all day Saturday?" Sarah's quiet question brought another rush of emotion, but Grace blinked to hold back the tears. She didn't have the energy to discuss Zach with Sarah.

"Let's not talk about that right now."

But Sarah repeated her question. "Where were you Saturday?"

Grace sighed. "I was with Zach. And Amos," she added.

Her memory replayed the stricken look on Zach's face when his uncle had revealed that Kinley was his daughter.

Now she shook her head, swallowing a hot knot in her throat. "No matter what you think of him, he's a good man now."

Sarah was silent. She was frowning, but not as fiercely as Grace had seen before.

And suddenly, she couldn't keep the words inside.

"Could you imagine if Isaiah was suddenly left alone, with no one to care for him? All our relatives, gone. What would happen if he was left with someone who didn't really care for him at all? Someone who never hugged him. Someone who treated him like a burden, not like a little boy."

She didn't know if her words were making any difference. Saying them aloud was a reminder of everything that Zach had been through. He had overcome his past, though it had taken him some trauma to get there. He was someone who deserved more than her half-hearted friendship.

She used her wrist to brush away one errant tear that had escaped. "I love you, Sarah. But I've begun to care about Zach, too. I didn't mean for it to happen, and I didn't do it to betray you. And now I don't know what to do."

Sarah didn't rail or gripe at her. For once, she remained silent and beside Grace as the morning wore on. This wasn't peace. Or acceptance.

But at least Sarah had listened.

Grace didn't tell her about Zach's daughter. That news was too private. And she didn't ask Sarah for her blessing. Sarah might never be able to forgive Zach.

But an aborted friendship wasn't enough for Grace anymore. She missed talking to Zach. She missed his smiles.

She missed him.

Zach missed supper.

It had already grown dark when he crossed the yard from the *daadi haus* to the big house. Someone was silhouetted in the kitchen window, and as he drew near, he saw it was Grace.

She was moving around slightly, and he real-ized she must be doing dishes.

His steps slowed. Maybe he shouldn't go in. But he needed to speak to Mr. Beiler. He sighed and kept going.

Inside the mudroom, he tried to steady him-self as he took off his coat. It didn't help.

When he crossed into the kitchen, he saw that he'd guessed right. Grace was wrist-deep in sudsy water, a dwindling stack of dirty dishes on the counter beside her. He could hear muted voices from deeper in the house.

She glanced over her shoulder at him, and he saw the lines around her mouth, as if she was tired or upset. The tip of her nose was pink.

He fought off the urge to go to her and ask what was wrong. That wasn't his place. He glanced away and glimpsed her father through the doorway. Mr. Beiler was reading a newspa-per with a cup of *kaffee* at the table.

Zach was moving that direction when Grace dried her hands on her apron and stepped to-ward him.

His emotions were too raw to talk to her. "I need to talk to your *daed*."

She threaded her fingers together in front of her waist. "Are you hungry? I can bring you a plate while you chat."

His stomach grumbled its agreement with

her plan, but he wasn't fit for company tonight. "What I have to say will only take a minute."

She opened her mouth as if she wanted to say more, but Isaiah clattered into the kitchen.

"That's the last of the dishes," her brother said cheerfully, unaware of the tension between them. "I'm going to check on the puppies." He brushed past Zach, only taking time to grab his coat from the hook.

Zach walked across the room and was almost to the threshold when Grace whispered, "Zach, wait. I—"

He hesitated on the threshold to the dining room, but Mr. Beiler looked up from his paper, and Zach's chance to speak with Grace alone was over. Maybe it was for the best.

Mr. Beiler nodded in greeting and invited Zach to sit down. He sat across the table from the older man, aware of the voices in the living room, aware of Grace moving around in the kitchen.

Zach didn't know where to start.

And suddenly, Grace was at his side, setting a plate heaped with meat loaf and mashed potatoes and green beans on the table in front of him. The scent of it made Zach's mouth water. How could he be hungry when it felt like all his insides were twisted into a pretzel?

"Thank you," he murmured.

Grace went back to the kitchen. He didn't have to look that direction to know she was hovering in the doorway. Listening.

What did it matter? There were other family members in the living room. The family was so big that there was no privacy to be found. It was like prison all over again. It shouldn't bother him, but it did.

He forced himself to recount this morning's phone call with his uncle. His knee bounced beneath the table, but at least Grace's father couldn't see the visible sign of his tension.

"After work, I went to see Kinley's mother."

Grace moved in the doorway, and he was distracted for a second.

"I thought maybe she would help—maybe talk to Paul for me. But she doesn't want anything to do with me or the situation."

Grace left the doorway and came to stand behind her *daed*'s shoulder. He had to avert his eyes from the compassion and concern in her expression. She'd seen Kinley at Paul's house. The girl needed better care.

His hands started shaking, and he fisted them on his thighs. "I can't stand the thought of her under his roof."

Mr. Beiler's brow furrowed, and he took off his glasses to lay them on top of the newspaper. "Will he hurt her?"

*Did he hurt you?*

Grace went very still. Almost as if his answer mattered to her.

Zach shook his head. "He never hit me."

"There are more ways to injure someone than with a fist," Grace said softly.

Zach's breath caught in his chest.

"What about taking him to court for custody?" she suggested. "Surely if we could prove neglect, she would be allowed to stay with Zach."

Mr. Beiler frowned. "Was she neglected?"

She hurried on, "We only saw Kinley for a few minutes, but her clothes didn't look clean or like they fit well. Her face was dirty, like she hadn't bathed in days."

And Paul had told her to pour herself a bowl of cereal. A child of three.

Zach flinched. He turned his face away for a moment, trying to hide the emotion that punched him.

Mr. Beiler passed a hand over his mouth. "We should talk to the bishop."

"Yes. Get the community behind Zach," Grace murmured.

Would that even work? The guys at the shop had begun to accept his overtures of friendship, but did that mean they would side with him?

But Mr. Beiler shook his head slowly. "I can guess what he will say. Our church doesn't believe in bringing a lawsuit against someone else."

Zach felt as if he'd been struck.

"Maybe he will be on Zach's side." But even Grace's hopeful statement sounded disbelieving.

"It isn't about taking sides," Mr. Beiler said. "Suing someone is the way the world solves problems. Not the way we solve them."

His hands went cold. He ducked his head, trying to stem his rising desperation.

"But you can still talk to the bishop, can't you?" she asked.

"*Jah*. We will go tomorrow, before work."

It was decided. There was nothing else he could do for now.

Zach excused himself and rose from the table. If he'd hoped to escape outside before Grace followed him, he was disappointed.

"Zach, wait."

He stopped, turning only halfway. It was easier not to face her completely.

She held the plate extended to him. "You didn't eat. You have to take care of yourself."

Her words were meant to be kind, but it was a reminder that he was alone. He had to take care of himself.

He thought about refusing her offer of kindness, but it was easier to take the plate.

She didn't let go immediately. She held on to

the edge of the plate until he looked up into her face. "I will pray for Kinley. It isn't fair, and there must be a way…"

He felt empty. "Even if the bishop grants permission for me to take my uncle to court, what judge would look at my history and award me custody?" He shook his head, despair engulfing him.

"You've proved yourself since your release," she argued.

"For only a matter of weeks."

He didn't know the workings of a family court. None of it looked good for him.

"Perhaps the prison could provide a letter about your behavior," she suggested. Now she was pulling at straws. Why wouldn't she give up? Why push now, when it was clear there was no future for them?

"I can't talk about this any longer," he said.

But she wasn't done. Her chin was stubbornly raised. "You have friends in Walnut Cove, Zach Miller. Don't forget."

*Friends.*

Her words sparked latent anger inside that he hadn't realized was simmering beneath the surface.

"It must be easy to say the words," he bit out. "But we both know you won't be standing beside me publicly."

She recoiled from the heated anger in his words, her hand coming to cover her mouth.

He knew it was unfair. He'd meant the words to hurt, and it was obvious by the shadows in her eyes that he'd accomplished it.

He shoved the plate into her hands and stalked out, afraid he would say more. Ashamed of wounding her.

For days, he'd been telling himself that he didn't care that she'd chosen Sarah. He even believed it.

But when she'd distanced herself from their budding relationship, he'd felt remnants of his childhood. The dawning awareness that no matter what he did, he wouldn't be good enough. The desperate wish for someone to belong to.

Grace might pretend she still had hope, but he had none left.

## *Chapter Nineteen*

Zach fumbled with the wrapping paper.

He was crouched on the floor of the post office, feeling every stare from the customers in line. It would've been better if he had thought ahead and bought these gifts for Kinley before today.

The quaint Amish gift shop had been packed with last-minute Christmas Eve shoppers searching for the perfect gift. The press of the crowd had forced Zach to fight off memories of too-close quarters with other inmates.

And he'd stood for too long looking at a display of Grace's violets with their showy flowers.

He missed her.

Eventually, he'd persevered and found what he sought. Now the post office was closing in a matter of minutes, and he needed to get his gifts wrapped and tucked inside the box he had waiting next to him.

But he couldn't remember wrapping gifts before and the paper was fragile, tearing when he pressed too hard against it. The tape was unwieldy, probably because his fingers were cold.

And he was second-guessing all this.

Amos had made an offhand comment that perhaps Zach should send Kinley a Christmas gift. He hadn't meant today. He'd said as much, suggesting Zach mail a gift early next week.

But as he'd worked several hours on this chilly Saturday morning in Mr. Beiler's shop, he couldn't stop thinking about Amos's idea. Mr. Beiler had put Zach in charge of the shop for the weekend half day. The Beiler family would host worship services tomorrow, and Mr. Beiler had wanted to be home to help prepare for the crowd that would descend on them tomorrow. But he'd committed to a firm deadline for the Culpeppers' barn and with an experienced team of workers, Mr. Beiler had counted on them to prepare several dozen framing boards.

The fact that he'd trusted Zach with the key to the shop had been a balm after a difficult week.

Amos's idea about sending Kinley a gift had taken hold of him, and he'd felt the need to do it now. She wouldn't receive the package until the day after Christmas, but at least it would be something.

And it would give him a few hours away from the *daadi haus* and the memories of Grace that dogged every step he took.

He hadn't been able to decide between a hand-sewn teddy bear or a wooden top that reminded him of the way he and Grace had spun together in the snow, weeks ago now. He'd also found a colorful children's book. He knew Kinley couldn't read yet. She was too young. Perhaps she might look at the pages and think of him.

That was, if Paul gave her the gifts at all.

He couldn't remember ever being excited about celebrating Christmas with his uncle. When his middle school friends had anticipated the holiday, he'd merely endured it. The time away from his school friends had felt like a punishment. Surely there had been at least one gift, but they had never had a tree, and he certainly had never received a special gift like a bicycle or anything like that.

Zach didn't know what his uncle would do when the package showed up in the mail. He could only pray the man would do the right thing and pass the gifts along to Kinley. Even if Paul took credit for them, Zach wouldn't care.

He wanted her to have a gift. That was more important than knowing Zach had sent it.

It hurt that he couldn't be with Kinley at this special time of year. He wanted to be with her every day, to know that she was safe and healthy. *Soon*, he prayed.

He finally got the last fold right and quickly taped the paper. It was ugly, but maybe a three-year-old wouldn't notice. He gently set the wrapped packages in the box and crinkled the paper bag he'd received when he had checked out from the store down the street. He used it as packing paper so the packages wouldn't move around once he closed the box.

He joined the back of the line, knowing he was going to have to wait as people mailed their last-minute packages.

He hadn't told anyone about this errand. Not even Amos when they'd parted ways at the shop.

He mailed his package and took a leisurely route home. It would take him past Mr. Beiler's shop. He was lost in his thoughts and almost missed seeing the commotion at the shop, which was set back from the main road.

He nearly crashed his bike, hitting the brakes too hard as he registered the two police cars in front of the shop. Their lights were on, flashing red and blue. From here he could see several buggies gathered. People were milling around outside the shop. What was going on?

Heart thrumming, he turned around and walked his bike up the street.

Before he had reached the tableau, he caught sight of a woman in a blue dress and dark apron, across the parking lot. She was standing with a police officer, and she pointed right at him. At this distance, he couldn't make out her features.

His hands were shaking as he rolled the bike to a stop. The woman disappeared inside the shop, but the police officer strode directly toward Zach.

Zach's stomach dropped, and he veered away, toward Reuben and someone Zach vaguely recognized with him. Maybe his mother, or an older sister. Zach had seen them together at worship. He needed to find out what was going on.

But the police officer intercepted him.

Zach felt himself react without consciously doing it. He adopted the slumped shoulders and ducked head, the same posture he had used whenever a guard approached while he was in prison. As if he was already beaten. The man was taller than Zach, with broad shoulders and a day's worth of scruff on his chin. He was uniformed, and Zach didn't want to think about the weapons on his belt.

"Zach!" Grace was there to witness his humiliation. Where had she come from? She was breathless and worried. "Where have you been?"

"Is this him, miss?" The police officer was talking to Grace, Zach realized.

"Yes, this is Zach Miller."

"What happened?" Zach asked the policeman.

Reuben and his sister were staring now, and so were an *Englisher* couple who had walked over from the quilting shop down the street. Zach edged away from Grace. He didn't wanted her touched by association with him.

"Someone broke into the shop," Grace said. She looked near tears. "They—"

"That's enough," the police officer snapped.

Grace shrank back at the hard tone in his voice.

Zach tried not to flinch.

"I need to question him before you can talk."

Zach's heart thundered as the police officer grabbed his upper arm. He didn't try to shake off the hold or resist in any way.

"I'm a suspect?" he asked.

Numbness was stealing over him, but not fast enough to stop the spear of pain when Grace rushed to say, "We didn't know where you were. Reuben's *mamm* saw someone with a bike like yours ride behind the shop. She sent Reuben over to check on things and—"

"That's enough." The officer's voice was sharp. He tugged Zach bodily away from Grace and toward one of the police cars.

The man didn't say anything as he ushered Zach to the vehicle. He opened the back door and motioned for Zach to get inside.

"I have an alibi," Zach stammered. He hated the weakness in his voice. He wasn't handcuffed, but he might as well have been. He felt trapped by the man's large body, the way he had herded Zach between the car door and the car itself.

Over his shoulder, he could see Grace standing in the open. She stared at him. He couldn't look at her.

"I'll ask you some questions in a minute. I need to grab my partner. Get in."

Zach couldn't disobey. He knew that would end badly for him.

He folded himself into the back of the car. The door closed, and he was locked inside, the sudden silence bearing down on him.

Grace was talking rapid-fire to Violet now, who'd joined her. She was motioning toward the car where he sat.

Did she really think him capable of vandalizing the shop?

The fragments of their broken friendship were jagged, cutting him up inside.

He didn't know what to think, what to feel right now. His terror at being in the back of a police car again brought flashes of memory of the night of the accident.

Grace had witnessed that, too.

*We both know you won't be standing beside me publicly.*

His words from days ago echoed in his mind.

Grace had been right to distance herself from him. He knew he was innocent, but because of his record the police were going to take some convincing. If they didn't believe him, he might be sent to jail.

Even if he was able to prove his innocence, the folks around here would be talking about him. Rumors would swirl. What woman would want her reputation tarnished by being his friend?

Not Grace.

Not anyone.

# *Chapter Twenty*

Zach was questioned by the police officer for half an hour. He explained exactly where he had been since he had left the shop after closing up. He tried to remember whether he had locked the shop door. He had. He was sure of it. Hopefully Amos could corroborate his memory.

He detailed everything he could remember about his time at the gift shop. He searched his memory for the faces of people he had encountered, only able to name the girl behind the counter who had checked him out because he had read her name tag.

Same thing with the post office. He was sure he had seen a familiar face or two in line, but he could only remember the name of the postal worker who had helped him with his transaction.

When he produced receipts for both his purchases and his postage, the officer had made notations in a small notebook and taken photos of Zach's receipts.

He seemed to believe Zach, at least as much as the evidence proved his innocence.

And then it was over. Or at least this part of it.

Zach was let out of the police cruiser. Amos jumped out of a buggy nearby and came toward him.

The sight of Amos's friendly face brought unshed tears to Zach's eyes.

"Are you okay?" Amos asked.

Zach shook his head. He was shaken and felt sick, but at least he wasn't going back to prison. Where was Mr. Beiler?

"What happened? Was anyone hurt?"

Amos shook his head. "Someone broke in and busted up the place. No one was here when it happened."

But the crew had left only a scant few hours ago. It had to have happened right after. Had someone been watching them? Waiting for them to leave?

It made Zach shudder to consider it.

He walked toward the shop. He shouldn't go in there, but he needed to see Grace. She'd been upset and trembling when the officer had interrupted her. Zach wouldn't get close to her. He just needed to see that she was all right.

"I think Violet took *Aendi* Beth home."

"Did Grace go with her?"

Zach only dimly registered that Amos was answering as he crossed the threshold into the shop. Someone had pried the door open with enough force to break the casing, which meant the officers' questions about Zach locking up hadn't mattered at all.

Inside, the shop was a wreck. Someone had knocked over the Culpeppers' timber, which had been stacked neatly in the center of the floor, ready to be loaded up in a few weeks' time when the barn would be constructed. It looked as if someone had taken one of the two-by-fours, or maybe multiple of them, and used them to bludgeon Mr. Beiler's machinery. The pneumatic saw was in pieces, strewn across the floor. A set of chisels had been pounded into some of the lumber with blunt force, as if someone was using them as nails instead of the tools they were. Whoever had done this had used spray paint to mark all over the lumber scattered across the floor.

Mr. Beiler exited the break room, accompanied by another uniformed officer. The officer seemed to be arguing with Mr. Beiler, who was shaking his head, wearing a firm frown.

The officer left without a word to Zach or Amos.

And then Mr. Beiler stood still, his gaze tracking around the shop.

"How can I help?" Zach asked.

Mr. Beiler looked surprised to see them there. Hadn't he noticed them? He appeared worn, defeated—an expression that Zach had never seen on the man before.

"The community will come together and help clean the place up," Amos offered. "We'll be swarmed first thing on Monday, as soon as everyone hears about it."

Mr. Beiler's jaw was tight. "Whoever did this, they ruined at least a week's worth of timber. But it's the tools that can't be replaced."

Zach had seen the community rally together to build the Troyers' house in a single day. Surely they would help replace Mr. Beiler's tools. But when he said as much, the older man shook his head. "Some of the chisels were passed down to me by my father, who had received them from his father. They are irreplaceable."

Compassion swirled. Grace had once told him about Mr. Beiler moving to Walnut Cove with his father. How they'd had only each other to rely on. And the bond they'd shared. Zach had envied him then. But he didn't envy Mr. Beiler's pain. He had to be devastated by the loss.

He realized that Mr. Beiler hadn't looked at him since he'd entered. Was he angry? He'd left the shop in Zach's hands. Did it matter that the vandalism had happened after Zach and the crew had left for the day? No. Guilt rose inside him, unchecked.

"I should've come straight home," he stammered. He felt more shaken now than he had when the officer had questioned him.

Since the day that Mr. Beiler had offered him a job, he'd done everything he could to exceed the man's expectations. He worked hard. He cleaned up after himself. He volunteered to stay late. Mr. Beiler and Amos were true friends, but the others were friends by association with the two men.

If he'd lost Mr. Beiler's regard…he didn't know what he'd do.

Or maybe he wouldn't have to do anything. Maybe Mr. Beiler would tell him it was time to move on.

The older man did none of that, just sighed. He still didn't look at Zach.

"It's time to go home. This is a problem for Monday morning. We still have much to do to get ready for tomorrow."

Zach and Amos followed him outside.

Across the parking lot, Grace was speaking to someone in a buggy. She apparently said her goodbyes, because whoever was in the buggy waved and then their buggy rolled off. She turned and caught sight of the three men.

She walked across the space, moving to hug her father when she came close. "*Mamm* couldn't seem to stop crying. I thought it was best to send Violet home with her in the second buggy."

"*Goot.*" But Mr. Beiler's voice didn't sound *goot.* "Let's go, then."

Grace glanced at Zach, and he saw the shadows behind her eyes. "*Daed*, I need to speak with Zach."

Mr. Beiler glanced at the waiting buggy. "You'll make sure she gets home?"

Zach started to answer, but then he saw the question was directed at Amos.

Amos jerked his thumb at the last buggy in the lot, the same one he'd climbed out of to check on Zach. "I can give Grace a ride."

Mr. Beiler nodded and then left.

Zach's emotions swirled in a dizzying maelstrom.

Grace was looking at him with a questioning gaze. "Where were you this afternoon?"

"In town."

He couldn't read her expression. Was she... suspicious of him?

"Did you have anything to do with this?"

What was she asking? She thought he'd been involved in the break-in?

Zach felt as if the world had shifted off its axis and he was left on shaky ground, with no foundation to stand on.

He pictured the mess inside the shop. It represented hundreds, if not thousands, of dollars of loss.

Grace thought him capable of that?

Grace had seen the stricken look on Zach's face when he had asked the police officer if he was a suspect.

This was somehow worse.

He looked as if she'd struck him.

"Zach, I have to know." She didn't want to think that Zach could do something like this, but he'd been so angry with her the last time they'd spoken.

He shook his head, his expression filled with disbelief.

Amos cleared his throat. "Do you want me to wait…?"

But Zach cut him off with a wave of his hand. "Stay."

She swallowed. She would rather have had this conversation without her cousin present, but she wasn't going to argue.

"How could you think I would break into

your *daed*'s shop? Did you see the damage? Your *daed* has been nothing but kind to me."

How could she explain what had happened? The paths her mind had taken?

"What was I supposed to think? No one knew where you were. Noah Bontrager knocked on the door and had a wild story about policemen being at the shop." Noah was Elijah's age. "He's got a reputation for telling tall tales, but he convinced us that something had happened, and we all piled in the wagons."

Zach stared at the building.

"When nobody could find you, I thought…" She'd thought the worst.

Zach flinched.

Amos shifted his feet. "I'm gonna go wait by the buggy—"

But Zach shook his head. "No." He took off his hat and pushed one hand through his hair. He turned away, tension in the line of his shoulders and the tightness in his back.

She'd been foolish. She'd seen the destruction in *Daed*'s shop and remembered Zach's anger. How his helplessness had made him fierce. She'd let Sarah's earlier words poison her thoughts.

And she'd had one moment of doubt.

"I made a mistake," she whispered. "I said something about you in front of one of the policemen, and he started asking questions." Questions *Mamm* had answered, hesitantly.

Zach stared out into the empty field behind the shop. She didn't know what he was thinking. Or if he would be able to forgive her.

"How did the police get involved?" Amos asked her.

"Reuben's *mamm* was in the quilt shop down the street. She saw someone ride a bike behind the shop and thought it looked suspicious. She sent Reuben over to check on things and he scared off the vandal, but not before all that damage was done."

Amos looked confused. "Did Reuben's *mamm* call the police?"

Grace shook her head. "The *Englisher* couple who run the quilt shop overheard them and called. I heard Reuben giving a description to the policeman."

Amos shook his head. "I heard him, too. Whoever did it was dressed like one of us."

But no one in their community would've done something so awful to *Daed*. Would they?

Grace had let Sarah's insidious whispers play in her ear. *Zach isn't what he seems.* She hadn't turned Grace against Zach, but she'd made her question. Just enough.

And Grace had let Zach down.

He still wouldn't look at her. "I'm really tired," he said finally.

"Can't we talk this out?" she asked.

"Is there anything left to talk about? You thought I could do that." He waved a disgusted hand at the shop.

She'd hurt him so badly.

"I need some time to think."

After everything, this was the only thing she could give him. She left with Amos in his buggy, sending a last look to the lost man pushing his bicycle away from *Daed*'s shop.

# Chapter Twenty-One

Grace was sitting between *Mamm* and her cousin Macy on the church bench when the men began filing into the basement. It was the Beilers' Sunday to host the worship service, and she'd been up since before dawn, helping *Mamm* get things set up and cleaned.

Grace couldn't help scanning each face as the bodies came down the stairs.

And finally, just before the younger boys clambered down the stairs like a herd of baby elephants, Zach entered.

He took his seat without looking in her direction, but she couldn't look away from him. He was pale and looked exhausted, lines bracketing his mouth. Had he slept at all? Where had he gone after he'd left *Daed*'s shop? She'd watched out her bedroom window, waiting to see him return. Her exhaustion from the emotional day forced her to go to bed before he had.

The only thing that mattered was that he was here. She still had a chance to make things right.

As voices raised in song around her, she knew she should be concentrating on the worship service, but she found herself distracted, unable to stop scrutinizing his face, looking for any sign of his hurt or any small sliver of hope he might have left.

He did not look her way once.

She was sorry for the way she'd treated him at the shop last night. And even before that, when she'd backed away from their relationship. She'd let her broken relationship with Sarah dictate her choices. She should've found a better way to reach Sarah. She cared about Zach, but she'd let her fears get in the way.

She forced herself to pay attention as Miriam's *daed* gave a long Christmas sermon about Jesus's birth. Hearing the familiar story sent ribbons of peace twining through her. Jesus had not come at a painless time. He was not delivered to a family that found it easy. He had come amid trouble and from humble beginnings and provided grace for the entire world.

She carried that sense of peace with her as worship ended. Maybe it was untoward, but she darted across the expanse between the women's and men's benches and approached Zach as he stood.

She hated the wariness in his eyes. And she was aware of numerous eyes on them. "I have to help *Mamm* set out the meal. But please don't leave. I need to talk to you."

He hesitated, his glance shifting around the room. "I don't think that's the best idea, Grace."

Her throat felt hot, and when he looked back at her, she saw the misery in his eyes. "Please. Zach."

He nodded, jaw tight. It would have to be enough for now.

She joined *Mamm* in the kitchen, along with Sarah and Violet. Macy and Esther followed her, and the six of them hurried to set out the meal. Sarah kept her head down, not talking to anyone. Right now, Grace had no words to speak to Sarah. Two relationships were broken. And she had to do what was right for both.

Friends and family began moving through the serving line. Mothers herding small children, young men chatting with each other about the possible snowfall this weekend. Esther and Macy made their plates and left the kitchen. A couple people expressed their condolences to *Mamm* about the burglary. Sarah tightened up both times, but Grace didn't understand why.

No one mentioned Zach. It was as if the church was holding its breath, unsure what to do with the situation. Grace panicked when the crowd began to thin and she hadn't seen Zach come through. Had he left, even though he'd said he would stay?

*Mamm* and Violet were adding food to their plates as Grace stepped into the dining room to look for him. There he was, standing with Amos in the corner. The older folks had gathered in the living room, but in here it was a mixture of teens and young adults. All Grace's friends. Miriam looked at her in concern. Reuben was shooting suspicious glances in Zach's direction.

Everyone knew what had happened last night. Maybe they even blamed Zach. And that wasn't right.

Neither Amos nor Zach held a plate, and they looked to be in serious discussion. No. Amos was speaking urgently while Zach stood stoic, hiding every bit of expression.

And Grace suddenly knew what she had to do. Nerves fluttered in her stomach and sent her pulse flying.

She cleared her throat, but only Miriam, sitting at the end of the table, heard her and looked up. What would it take to get everyone's attention? She let out a whistle, one she might've used to call Bertha outside.

Instant silence descended. Her face flamed. "You've all heard by now about *Daed*'s shop being burglarized. Maybe some of you heard that the police questioned Zach. But I want you to know that Zach is innocent." It didn't matter that she didn't know who'd done it. She knew who *hadn't*.

Zach's stare landed on her. She kept her eyes locked on him from across the room. His expression was inscrutable. He even shook his head slightly.

She raised her chin, not looking away from him. "Zach has become a dear friend to me." So much more than that. "I care about him a great deal."

Zach mouthed her name. His carefully neutral expression broke just enough that she saw a flash of emotion.

She let her eyes sweep over her friends at the table. "Zach had nothing to do with what happened at *Daed*'s shop. You can trust me on that."

Past Zach and Amos, she could see *Daed* standing in the dining room doorway. He'd obviously overheard everything.

Whispers broke out at the table as she turned and swept back into the kitchen. Violet slipped past her, wide-eyed. *Mamm* stood near the sink, her plate abandoned on the counter. Sarah must have fled upstairs.

Why were her eyes burning? She brushed the tears away.

Footsteps sounded behind her. More than one pair of feet.

When she turned, *Daed* moved past her into the room, and as he stepped out of the way she saw Zach standing uncertainly inside the doorway.

She smiled at him, because she would always be glad to see him. A tear fell, and she brushed it away impatiently.

He stepped toward her and reached out his hand. So many times, it had been Grace initiating contact between them. Taking his hand, touching his arm.

She'd wondered if he'd been afraid to touch her. Or maybe unsure whether his touch would be welcome.

But he reached for her now, and she eagerly took his hand. The feeling of his fingers sliding against hers was both a relief and a promise.

She took the first deep breath since she'd left *Daed*'s shop last night.

Zach's throat was hot. He wanted to cry. He also wanted to shout.

Grace had stood up for him. She cared about him.

The way she was looking at him now…

His feelings for her felt as if they were bursting from his skin, too big to hold inside.

He had so many things to say to her.

But her *daed* and *mamm* were here, watching. Mr. Beiler had been good to him, and he deserved to hear it from Zach.

He looked Mr. Beiler straight in the eye. "I didn't break into the shop, and I didn't wreck the machinery. It's all right if you can't believe me or if you don't want to keep me on."

He didn't actually know what he'd do if he didn't have a job. Start over again.

"I'm not leaving Walnut Cove." Until a few minutes ago, he'd planned just the opposite. Amos had argued with him in a fierce, low voice. He'd urged Zach to talk to Mr. Beiler. To talk to Grace.

And Zach would regret it every day of his life if he walked away from her.

"It's my fault." A quiet voice from the doorway, behind Zach, spoke up.

Zach twisted, and Grace moved so that she could see past him, though she didn't let go of him.

Sarah.

"What are you talking about?" Mr. Beiler's voice cracked like a whip.

Sarah looked over her shoulder. Voices in the

dining room behind her were a reminder that anyone could overhear them.

"Maybe we should speak somewhere else." Grace's *mamm* had a sound idea, and the five of them hurried across the yard to the *daadi haus*.

Inside, Zach and Grace crossed behind the tiny kitchen island and stood facing her parents and sister. Sarah looked worn-out and empty. Her face was drawn and pale.

"Did you break into the shop?" Mr. Beiler asked.

Sarah shook her head, but then nodded miserably. She swiped at a tear falling down her cheek. "It wasn't—wasn't supposed to happen like that. I paid him to spray paint the outside of the building. It would've been easy to paint over." Her voice trembled. "I didn't know he was going to bust down the door or break your machines. I didn't know."

*Sarah* had been behind the break-in. She'd known the police would look at Zach first, because of his past.

Sarah had a right to be angry. But that didn't stop the hurt that rose to choke him.

"Why?" Mr. Beiler demanded.

But Zach knew, even before she spoke. She hated him.

But she didn't say the words. She dissolved into tears, her hands coming over her face.

Grace looked as shell-shocked as he felt. He'd never expected this confession. He felt as if the earth had shifted beneath his feet. Sarah had caused the damage to her family's business.

But it was so obvious that she was hurting.

Grace let go of him to go to her sister. She joined her *mamm* and put her arms around Sarah as she cried. Mr. Beiler watched with a deep frown on his face.

"You were r-right," Sarah said through her sobs. She was talking to Grace. "Thomas would've been so ashamed of me. I'm ashamed of me. I just wanted him back. I want him back."

Her tears overcame her again.

Grace looked up at Zach, and his hurt twisted inside his stomach.

Did he have a right to judge Sarah when he'd been the one to hurt her so badly in the first place? It was a convoluted mess. And being angry with her would only make it worse.

Mr. Beiler turned to Zach, unsmiling. "I need to apologize to you, *sohn*. Last night, I blamed you unjustly. I wasn't thinking clearly." He shook his head. "That is not an excuse. I ask your forgiveness."

Zach's throat was hot and raw. "I forgive you." How could he do any different, when he'd been forgiven so much?

Sarah looked up at Grace. "Days ago, when

you were weeping in the greenhouse, I began to realize what Zach meant to you. And I thought about what it would be like if Thomas were alive and someone was treating him the way I treated Zach." Her tearstained gaze shifted to connect with Zach's. "I'm sorry. I'm so sorry."

It was the first moment she'd really seen him. He saw the recognition in her eyes. They were both broken. But they didn't have to stay that way. Like Grace's flowers, they could grow whole again.

"I'm sorry, too," he said.

Her head bowed, as if his words were too heavy to bear.

Grace hugged her sister once more and left her in her *mamm*'s embrace. She returned to Zach's side.

Mr. Beiler went to take Grace's place beside Sarah. He laid a hand on her back. "There will be consequences for this. I'll have to speak to the bishop." He inhaled sharply. "We'll be behind on completing the barn for the Culpeppers. The destroyed wood will have to be replaced. And the machinery…"

Zach spoke up. "I can fix the saw. It might take days to get the parts we need, since it's a holiday. But I saw the damage last night, and it can be mended."

Mr. Beiler wasn't usually one for showing

emotion, but Zach clearly saw his mentor's relief and gratefulness.

"I'm sure you and Grace need to talk."

Yes. They did.

Grace squeezed his hand tightly as her parents and sister took their leave.

He still felt an emptiness inside, in the spot reserved for Kinley. But he was overflowing with blessings.

And then he and Grace were alone.

He turned toward her to find her eyes uncertain.

"I'm sorry I let Sarah come between us," she said softly.

"She's your sister. How could you choose someone like me? Grace, I—" He shook his head. "I can't believe you did that." He motioned toward the house. "In there."

She was blushing now, but she didn't drop her gaze. "I'm sorry if that was too forward. Or if I embarrassed you in front of our friends."

"Your friends," he said. "And I wasn't embarrassed. I was honored."

"Our friends," she said with a soft emphasis. Now she did glance down, and he was aware of the short distance between them. "I'm sorry that I doubted you last night."

It had almost broken him. But… "It's no more

than I should expect, with the bad choices I made."

She shook her head and her eyes were sparkling with tears. "You should be able to expect more from the people who love you."

Her words made everything inside him cinch tight. He tried to breathe through the pounding of his pulse in his ears. She'd said the word *love*, but she hadn't said she loved him.

Before this morning, he wouldn't have dared to dream that she could.

But her courage had given him wings.

He shifted closer and raised his hand to brush the pad of his thumb across her cheek, catching her tears. "Grace, I think about you all the time. You're beautiful and you live up to your name, graceful and gentle. How could I not fall in love with you?"

Hope nearly strangled him, and he had to close his eyes against it. He tipped his forehead against hers and closed his eyes, just breathing in the sugar-apple scent of her.

"I love you," she whispered, her words a breath against his cheek.

Joy burst through him like the sun breaking through a cloud bank. She loved him. He'd hoped that someday—maybe years from now—he could prove himself and earn her love. Her words soaked into the thirsty desert of his heart, filling cracks he hadn't even known existed.

And she'd given it to him freely.

"I love you, too," he whispered. "I never thought…"

They stayed like that, with their foreheads touching, for a moment before she shifted even closer and rested her chin against his shoulder. His arms came around her, and they fit perfectly in each other's arms.

"I don't know what will happen with Kinley," he said quietly.

"*Gott* will protect her until she can come to live with you. And then we'll deal with whatever comes. Together."

He squeezed her gently.

Grace had burst into his life so unexpectedly and filled his days with joy and warmth and caring.

He cupped her cheek, and at the same moment, she raised her face to receive his kiss. Their lips met in a kiss that was a promise for today and for all their tomorrows. There were so many unknowns in his life, but he would have Grace at his side as he faced each new challenge. He loved her deeply, and he was never going to let her go.

## Chapter Twenty-Two

The morning of his wedding dawned bright and cold. It had been a little over a month since Zach's Christmas miracle—Grace loved him.

In his bedroom, he donned his suit coat and straightened his cuffs.

He had spent nearly every evening with Grace. Sometimes with her family. Sometimes he was allowed to drive the family buggy so that they could be alone for a short while.

After Grace's public declaration, the families in Walnut Cove had given him a warmer welcome than before. He'd gone to all the singings and had been surrounded by new friendships. He'd been invited to game nights at Amos's home. He'd learned to play Monopoly and another complicated board game that he had a knack for winning.

He and Sarah would probably never be close,

but she and Grace had patched up their relationship. Sarah would be one of Grace's attendants at their wedding, along with her other sisters.

In only a few hours, he and Grace would be married. And after that, Grace would move into the *daadi haus* with him. He hoped to save enough money in the next few months for them to move into a place of their own, but Grace's family insisted there was no rush.

It had taken Zach two weeks to repair the saw and other machinery at the shop. He and the other guys had worked overtime to complete the Culpepper job, and they'd barely finished on time.

Mr. Beiler was pleased with Zach's leadership and had let him take a prominent role in the barn raising. Zach had finally found a place he belonged.

A few months ago, Zach never would have thought that he would have this kind of peace and contentment. He had a community surrounding him, a family in the Beilers, and Grace by his side. He had a job that he loved and a future.

The only thing missing was Kinley.

Paul had allowed two weekend visits. Kinley knew who Zach was. They'd played Candyland, and he'd unobtrusively checked the pantry. He'd sent Paul money for groceries and had prayed that his uncle would use the money for food. Every time Zach had mentioned bringing Kinley home to Walnut Cove, Paul had refused. Each night he prayed for a miracle.

He gave one last glance to the gardening stool he'd crafted for Grace as a wedding gift. It stood proudly beneath the window where he kept the violet she'd given him months ago. It was in full bloom, pink flowers a constant reminder of her words from months ago. Something broken could be made whole again.

He was ready. More than ready to take Grace as his wife.

It was time to join Grace. They would meet with the bishop this morning during the worship service, and their wedding would take place directly after.

He stepped outside the *daadi haus* into bright winter sunshine, just as a car came up the drive.

It was early yet, and other families hadn't begun to arrive for worship. There wasn't a buggy in sight. Who was driving up to the house right now?

The older-model sedan drove slowly up to the house and stopped.

Zach squinted. Was that…?

It was Paul behind the wheel.

His uncle got out of the car. The older man

approached Zach where he stood frozen in front of the *daadi haus*.

Zach watched him warily. Was he here to cause trouble before the wedding?

"I brought Kinley."

Zach's throat closed up. How had Paul known about the wedding? And who had convinced him to bring Zach's daughter to witness it? Surely he wouldn't have been considerate enough to decide to come on his own.

Paul didn't look particularly happy to be here.

"Thank you," Zach said, voice hoarse. He didn't want to press his luck, but… "Can she stay for a few days?"

Paul frowned. "I thought Tiffany would've told you. I brought her to stay."

He *what*?

Zach was aware that Grace and Isaiah were now standing on the front stoop of the house, watching. It was so quiet that they could probably hear everything.

"Tiffany said your girlfriend talked to her. Two weeks ago."

Paul had to be talking about Grace. When had she gone to see Tiffany? She hadn't breathed a word.

"I guess she turned Tiffany into a bleeding heart. She said that she'd sic her lawyer on me if I didn't hand over Kinley to you."

He stood in stunned silence even as Paul glared at him. "You've always caused me trouble, kid. I don't need the drama in my life. So here she is."

*I don't need the drama.* This was more familiar to Zach than when he'd suspected Paul was being kind.

Paul was apparently finished talking, because he went to the back door of the sedan and opened it.

Zach couldn't tear his gaze away as Kinley hopped out of the car. She clutched a small, shabby suitcase and stood next to the car, staring at him.

His throat was clogged with emotion. He'd been praying for so long, never allowing himself to hope. He swallowed hard and looked at Paul. It no longer mattered that the old man had held himself distant from a boy who desperately needed love. All Zach could see was a beaten-down man who wanted life to be easy for him. Zach had a mentor and friend in Mr. Beiler, and he didn't have to question his worth anymore.

"Thank you."

His uncle shrugged off the words.

Zach didn't care. He crossed to Kinley and squatted down so he was at her level. "Hi."

"Hi." Her lashes fluttered as she glanced at him and back at the ground. She wasn't smiling.

He wasn't kidding himself that this was going to be easy. They didn't know each other. Not really. A few sporadic visits weren't enough. But he loved her so deeply. And he wanted to be the father she needed.

"I know you're probably scared. But I want you to know that I love you. I loved you from the minute I found out about you, and I'm never going to stop."

She blinked up at him, and the vulnerability in her eyes stole his breath.

Paul moved to get in the car. Kinley stood too close to the vehicle for Zach's comfort, and he held out his hand. She took it, and he led her away as the car roared to life.

Grace approached from the direction of the barn. He hadn't even realized she'd left the porch. She had Libby in her arms, a squirming, wiggling puppy-shaped distraction.

Beside him, Kinley lit up. She didn't even notice when Paul drove away.

Grace always knew the right thing to do.

She sat on the step.

"You remember Grace, don't you?" he asked Kinley.

"This is Libby," Grace said.

His daughter reached for the puppy, who came into her arms with a wildly wagging tail.

The puppy licked her chin, and his daughter giggled. Was there any better sound in the world?

Grace smiled tenderly, first at Kinley and then at Zach.

"How did you…?"

She knew what he was asking.

"Amos and I went to the gas station. We weren't there long. I think—" *Tiffany*, she mouthed over Kinley's head "—was already regretting your last conversation. She was very receptive when I told her how much you loved Kinley and wanted to care for her."

She shrugged, as if her actions hadn't totally changed his world.

Kinley's presence would change everything. It had changed from a *someday, maybe* to a *right now*. She would need a lot of care, and he would be thrown into the role of father without any preparation.

But he couldn't have asked for a better wedding gift.

Grace gave him a peaceful smile, not in a rush to go back inside, though he knew she must have a dozen prewedding tasks to complete. She was content to be with him and Kinley.

And he knew that whatever was to come, they would face it together.

\* \* \* \* \*

Dear Reader,

I love to garden. In late winter and early spring I am always waiting for the first green shoots to show up. That's one reason I love African violets: they are an easy houseplant that blooms all year long. Even during those long, dreary winter months.

I started growing violets as a teenager and I still love them now, decades later. My kitchen windowsill is overflowing with violets and my oldest daughter has started propagating her own from a leaf. One of the amazing things about these violets is that if they become damaged, they don't perish. You can grow a whole new plant from a single leaf.

In this book, Zach has experienced some major damage in his life. But God wasn't done with him; he is able to "grow" into a new life filled with friendship and love. Sometimes life happens, but God can always grow us into someone He can use.

I hope you enjoyed this book! Send me a note at lacy@lacywilliams.net, or you can send physical mail to: Lacy Williams, 340 S Lemon Ave #1639, Walnut, CA 91789.

Until next time, happy reading.
*Lacy*

# Get 4 FREE REWARDS!

## We'll send you 2 FREE Books plus 2 FREE Mystery Gifts.

**Love Inspired** books feature uplifting stories where faith helps guide you through life's challenges and discover the promise of a new beginning.

**FREE** Value Over **$20**

**YES!** Please send me 2 FREE Love Inspired Romance novels and my 2 FREE mystery gifts (gifts are worth about $10 retail). After receiving them, if I don't wish to receive any more books, I can return the shipping statement marked "cancel." If I don't cancel, I will receive 6 brand-new novels every month and be billed just $5.24 each for the regular-print edition or $5.99 each for the larger-print edition in the U.S., or $5.74 each for the regular-print edition or $6.24 each for the larger-print edition in Canada. That's a savings of at least 13% off the cover price. It's quite a bargain! Shipping and handling is just 50¢ per book in the U.S. and $1.25 per book in Canada.* I understand that accepting the 2 free books and gifts places me under no obligation to buy anything. I can always return a shipment and cancel at any time. The free books and gifts are mine to keep no matter what I decide.

Choose one: ☐ **Love Inspired Romance
Regular-Print**
(105/305 IDN GNWC)

☐ **Love Inspired Romance
Larger-Print**
(122/322 IDN GNWC)

Name (please print)

Address                                                                                    Apt. #

City                                    State/Province                        Zip/Postal Code

**Email:** Please check this box ☐ if you would like to receive newsletters and promotional emails from Harlequin Enterprises ULC and its affiliates. You can unsubscribe anytime.

Mail to the **Harlequin Reader Service:**
**IN U.S.A.:** P.O. Box 1341, Buffalo, NY 14240-8531
**IN CANADA:** P.O. Box 603, Fort Erie, Ontario L2A 5X3

Want to try 2 free books from another series! Call 1-800-873-8635 or visit www.ReaderService.com.

*Terms and prices subject to change without notice. Prices do not include sales taxes, which will be charged (if applicable) based on your state or country of residence. Canadian residents will be charged applicable taxes. Offer not valid in Quebec. This offer is limited to one order per household. Books received may not be as shown. Not valid for current subscribers to Love Inspired Romance books. All orders subject to approval. Credit or debit balances in a customer's account(s) may be offset by any other outstanding balance owed by or to the customer. Please allow 4 to 6 weeks for delivery. Offer available while quantities last.

**Your Privacy**—Your information is being collected by Harlequin Enterprises ULC, operating as Harlequin Reader Service. For a complete summary of the information we collect, how we use this information and to whom it is disclosed, please visit our privacy notice located at corporate.harlequin.com/privacy-notice. From time to time we may also exchange your personal information with reputable third parties. If you wish to opt out of this sharing of your personal information, please visit readerservice.com/consumerschoice or call 1-800-873-8635. **Notice to California Residents**—Under California law, you have specific rights to control and access your data. For more information on these rights and how to exercise them, visit corporate.harlequin.com/california-privacy.                                    LIR21R2

# Get 4 FREE REWARDS!

## We'll send you 2 FREE Books <u>plus</u> 2 FREE Mystery Gifts.

**Harlequin Heartwarming Larger-Print** books will connect you to uplifting stories where the bonds of friendship, family and community unite.

**FREE** Value Over **$20**

**YES!** Please send me 2 FREE Harlequin Heartwarming Larger-Print novels and my 2 FREE mystery gifts (gifts worth about $10 retail). After receiving them, if I don't wish to receive any more books, I can return the shipping statement marked "cancel." If I don't cancel, I will receive 4 brand-new larger-print novels every month and be billed just $5.74 per book in the U.S. or $6.24 per book in Canada. That's a savings of at least 21% off the cover price. It's quite a bargain! Shipping and handling is just 50¢ per book in the U.S. and $1.25 per book in Canada.* I understand that accepting the 2 free books and gifts places me under no obligation to buy anything. I can always return a shipment and cancel at any time. The free books and gifts are mine to keep no matter what I decide.

161/361 HDN GNPZ

Name (please print)

Address                                                                 Apt. #

City                                  State/Province                   Zip/Postal Code

Email: Please check this box ☐ if you would like to receive newsletters and promotional emails from Harlequin Enterprises ULC and its affiliates. You can unsubscribe anytime.

### Mail to the Harlequin Reader Service:
**IN U.S.A.:** P.O. Box 1341, Buffalo, NY 14240-8531
**IN CANADA:** P.O. Box 603, Fort Erie, Ontario L2A 5X3

Want to try 2 free books from another series! Call 1-800-873-8635 or visit www.ReaderService.com.

*Terms and prices subject to change without notice. Prices do not include sales taxes, which will be charged (if applicable) based on your state or country of residence. Canadian residents will be charged applicable taxes. Offer not valid in Quebec. This offer is limited to one order per household. Books received may not be as shown. Not valid for current subscribers to Harlequin Heartwarming Larger-Print books. All orders subject to approval. Credit or debit balances in a customer's account(s) may be offset by any other outstanding balance owed by or to the customer. Please allow 4 to 6 weeks for delivery. Offer available while quantities last.

**Your Privacy**—Your information is being collected by Harlequin Enterprises ULC, operating as Harlequin Reader Service. For a complete summary of the information we collect, how we use this information and to whom it is disclosed, please visit our privacy notice located at corporate.harlequin.com/privacy-notice. From time to time we may also exchange your personal information with reputable third parties. If you wish to opt out of this sharing of your personal information, please visit readerservice.com/consumerschoice or call 1-800-873-8635. **Notice to California Residents**—Under California law, you have specific rights to control and access your data. For more information on these rights and how to exercise them, visit corporate.harlequin.com/california-privacy.

HW21R2

# HARLEQUIN SELECTS COLLECTION

19 FREE BOOKS IN ALL!

**From Robyn Carr to RaeAnne Thayne to Linda Lael Miller and Sherryl Woods we promise (actually, GUARANTEE!) each author in the Harlequin Selects collection has seen their name on the *New York Times* or *USA TODAY* bestseller lists!**

---

**YES!** Please send me the **Harlequin Selects Collection**. This collection begins with 3 FREE books and 2 FREE gifts in the first shipment. Along with my 3 free books, I'll also get 4 more books from the Harlequin Selects Collection, which I may either return and owe nothing or keep for the low price of $24.14 U.S./$28.82 CAN. each plus $2.99 U.S./$7.49 CAN. for shipping and handling per shipment*.If I decide to continue, I will get 6 or 7 more books (about once a month for 7 months) but will only need to pay for 4. That means 2 or 3 books in every shipment will be FREE! If I decide to keep the entire collection, I'll have paid for only 32 books because 19 were FREE! I understand that accepting the 3 free books and gifts places me under no obligation to buy anything. I can always return a shipment and cancel at any time. My free books and gifts are mine to keep no matter what I decide.

☐ 262 HCN 5576 ☐ 462 HCN 5576

Name (please print)

Address                                                                                    Apt. #

City                                  State/Province                          Zip/Postal Code

Mail to the **Harlequin Reader Service:**
**IN U.S.A.:** P.O. Box 1341, Buffalo, NY 14240-8531
**IN CANADA:** P.O. Box 603, Fort Erie, Ontario L2A 5X3

*Terms and prices subject to change without notice. Prices do not include sales taxes, which will be charged (if applicable) based on your state or country of residence. Canadian residents will be charged applicable taxes. Offer not valid in Quebec. All orders subject to approval. Credit or debit balances in a customer's account(s) may be offset by any other outstanding balance owed by or to the customer. Please allow 3 to 4 weeks for delivery. Offer available while quantities last. © 2020 Harlequin Enterprises ULC. ® and ™ are trademarks owned by Harlequin Enterprises ULC.

**Your Privacy**—Your information is being collected by Harlequin Enterprises ULC, operating as Harlequin Reader Service. To see how we collect and use this information visit https://corporate.harlequin.com/privacy-notice. From time to time we may also exchange your personal information with reputable third parties. If you wish to opt out of this sharing of your personal information, please visit www.readerservice.com/consumerschoice or call 1-800-873-8635. Notice to California Residents—Under California law, you have specific rights to control and access your data. For more information visit https://corporate.harlequin.com/california-privacy.

50BOOKHS22R

# COMING NEXT MONTH FROM
## Love Inspired

### THE MIDWIFE'S CHRISTMAS WISH
*Secret Amish Babies* • by Leigh Bale
When Amish midwife Lovina Albrecht finds an abandoned baby in her buggy at Christmas, the bishop assigns her and brooding Jonah Lapp to care for it until the mother's found. But when a temporary arrangement begins to feel like family, can they overcome old hurts to build a future?

### HER SECRET AMISH MATCH
by Cathy Liggett
After Hannah Miller loses her dream job, her only option is to become a nanny—and matchmaker—for widower Jake Burkholder, the man who broke her heart when he married her best friend. But as secrets from the past are revealed, Hannah can't help but wonder if *she's* Jake's perfect match.

### HER CHRISTMAS DILEMMA
by Brenda Minton
Returning home for the holidays after an attack, Clara Fisher needs a fresh start—and working as a housekeeper for Tucker Church and his teenage niece is the first step. She still has hard choices to make about her future, but Tucker might just help her forget her fears...

### THEIR YULETIDE HEALING
*Bliss, Texas* • by Mindy Obenhaus
Foster mom Rae Girard is determined to give her children the best Christmas they've ever had—and she's shocked when the town scrooge, attorney Cole Heinsohn, offers to pitch in. But after tragedy strikes, could an imperfect holiday be just what they need to bring them all together...forever?

### OPENING HIS HOLIDAY HEART
*Thunder Ridge* • by Renee Ryan
The last thing Casey Evans wants is to be involved in a Christmas contest, but Mayor Sutton Wentworth insists she needs his coffee shop to participate. And when her son draws him into holiday festivities, Casey can't resist the little boy—or his mother. Can they thaw the walls Casey's built around his heart?

### A SMALL-TOWN CHRISTMAS CHALLENGE
*Widow's Peak Creek* • by Susanne Dietze
Selling the historic house she inherited would solve all of Leah Dean's problems—but first, she must work with her co-inheritor, Benton Hunt, to throw one last big Christmas party in the home. Yet as the holidays draw closer, saying goodbye to the house—and each other—might not be that easy.

---

**LOOK FOR THESE AND OTHER LOVE INSPIRED BOOKS WHEREVER BOOKS ARE SOLD, INCLUDING MOST BOOKSTORES, SUPERMARKETS, DISCOUNT STORES AND DRUGSTORES.**